MINOTAUR COUNTRY

Also by Helen McCloy

MINOTAUR COUNTRY

A Novel of Suspense

HELEN McCLOY

DODD, MEAD & COMPANY · NEW YORK

Library of Congress Cataloging in Publication Data

McCloy, Helen.
    Minotaur country.

    I. Title.
PZ3.M13358Mg   [PS3525.A1587]   813'.5'2   74–28370
ISBN 0–396–07004–3

To Halliday Dresser with love

Contents

There are other things, animals crashing around in the forest. I can hear them, but I can't see them.

—Senator Howard Baker,
December 30th, 1973.

PART I

Leafy Way

1

It was a Border state between North and South on the Eastern seaboard, embracing ten thousand square miles. It had been one of the thirteen original colonies, but not one of the eleven Confederate states. It had nineteen counties, one great university, and one good newspaper. Tatiana Perkins worked for the newspaper.

She was named Tatiana because her artist father admired the heroine of *Eugene Onyegin*. The moment she began to talk she called herself "Tash," and she had been Tash ever since.

By the time she was twelve, her parents were divorced. They still loved each other and Tash, but her father was in love with someone else. She heard him explain it to her mother:

"I didn't want this to happen. Try to think of me as if I had been driving a rickety car too fast on a rough mountain road."

That was when Tash decided that she herself would never fall in love.

No rickety cars on rough mountain roads for her. She liked men, but she did not like the havoc of passion. She was going to be happy.

Tash's father went to live in Rome with a mistress he

3

couldn't marry because of her Catholic conscience. Tash's mother settled in Boston with a new husband, the last green shoot on old, dry, Brahmin stock.

Tash herself did not feel at home in either household. When she left college, she drifted to the capital city of the Border state.

She had trouble getting a job because she looked so much younger than she actually was. She had the half-starved face of a street urchin: big eyes sunk too deep, thin cheeks too hollow, wide mouth too thin-lipped.

She finally landed her newspaper job because there happened to be a vacancy when she applied. She was soon trapped on the Women's Page, which bored her. One day she chanced to read a new novel advertised as "excitingly different" and "daringly original."

Oh, if only she were a book reviewer! She let off steam pounding out on her office typewriter the review she might have written.

A copy boy assumed it was for publication. A makeup man slid it into a slot on the daily book review page between two small ads. It glided past copy readers and assistant book editors without being noticed, and no one else saw it before publication. Next morning a furious book editor-in-chief asked the managing editor to fire Tash.

The managing editor refused.

"It was the copy boy's mistake, not hers. I've read the book. It's all she says and worse. I'm going to take her off the Women's Page. She needs more scope."

Two years later Tash had a syndicated column under her own byline and license to write about anything she pleased from sport to politics.

The first time she appeared as a guest on a television show, the producer gasped. "Isn't there anything—*anything*—you can do about your hair?"

She tossed the tangled, black mop out of her eyes and said, "No."

In a week the "mop cut" was all over town.

So she had done exactly what she set out to do. She had made a safe, little niche for herself in a brutally competitive world by her own efforts, and she had not fallen in love with anybody.

She was sitting at her desk one cold, sunny morning in April when a copy boy told her that the Old Man wanted to see her.

"Hi, Tash!" The managing editor, Bill Brewer, leaned back in the scruffy, swivel chair he cherished, both hands clasped behind his neck. "I'm going to make you mad."

"You couldn't."

"Oh, yes, I could. I'm going to ask you to do one more story for the Women's Page. An interview."

Tash gritted her teeth. "When ICBMs are falling, will you ask me for five hundred words on annhilation from the woman's point of view?"

"Our readers would love it."

Tash sighed. "All right. Who am I to interview? Miss Hayseed, 1956? Or the champion chicken-fryer of Backwoods County?"

"Neither. What do you know about Vivian Playfair?"

"The Governor's wife?" Tash whistled, an accomplishment she had cultivated ever since she was told as a child that whistling girls and crowing hens never come to very good ends.

"You seem impressed."

"I am. She never gives interviews."

"What else do you know about her?"

"She and the Governor are a matched pair. They have everything that most people want: health, youth, looks, power, position, money. All but one thing: children.

5

What makes you think she's willing to be interviewed now?"

"I met the Governor's aide, Carlos de Miranda, at a party last night. He finessed the idea that I should send someone to interview her this afternoon."

"Finessed?"

"He made the suggestion so adroitly that I thought it was my own suggestion until I had time to think it over."

"Why would he do that?"

"That's one of the things I'd like to find out. Maybe you can find out for me this afternoon."

"I doubt it. An interview with a woman like that has to be the usual guff. How she looks, how she dresses, how she plans menus and guest lists, and how strongly she feels that the wife of of a man in public life should give him every moral support while keeping herself modestly in the background. I could write it without going near her. A computer could write it. Even a good electric typewriter could write it. It writes itself."

"Tash, I want more than the usual guff. That's why I'm sending you."

"Thank you kindly, sir."

"I want to know why she is giving an interview for the first time. I want to know why Carlos de Miranda went out of his way to plant the idea of this interview in my mind. Is he trying to establish something? Or leak something? Or cover up something?"

"Would he leak something through the Governor's wife?"

"Probably not, but he might use an interview with her to distract attention from something else."

Bill's gaze went to the window where he could see the gilded dome of the State House above the tree tops along the Mall. "Do you know why I got this job? Because I have what they call a 'nose' for news. I feel things in my bones before they happen and now my bones are telling me that something is going to happen over there. I don't know what it is, but I can feel it."

Tash let the silence grow a moment, and then said: "What is it you haven't told me yet?"

"She disappears."

"Vivian Playfair?"

"Yes."

"Often?"

"Three times in the last year. The boys on the State House beat think she leaves town, but no announcements are made about her going away, and she's never seen in airports or railway stations. Even her car stays in the garage when she's . . . invisible."

"She could be ill."

"It would leak to the papers fast enough if a doctor were making regular visits or if she were in a hospital, but there's nothing. Not even a rumor. She just . . . isn't there."

"But he is?"

"Oh, yes. Whatever she does, she does alone."

"Now you're getting me interested. What time am I supposed to see her?"

"Three o'clock."

"I'll need a photographer."

"Take Sam."

Tash rose. To her surprise, Bill rose, too, and walked over to the elevator with her. Busy newspaper editors cannot often spare time for minor courtesies.

When the elevator door started to shut automatically, Bill stayed it with one hand. "Tash . . ."

"Yes?"

"Don't do anything foolish."

"What do you mean? Is there something more you haven't told me?"

"Nothing I can put into words, but . . . be careful."

2

ABOUT THE TIME people started calling the President's House in Washington the White House, the Governor's House in this state became known as Leafy Way, the name of the road where it stood at the edge of the capital city.

It was a winding road where tree branches met overhead to form a natural tunnel. On a spring day like this, the pavement was freckled with sun patches and leaf shadows that danced in each vagabond breeze.

They came suddenly to two brick pillars linked by carriage gates and an archway of wrought iron. Each pillar was crowned with a lantern of glass set in a rococo iron frame. A third lantern dangled from the apex of the arch.

"No brick walls? No electrified wire fences?" said Tash to Sam Bates, the photographer, who had often been here before.

"No," said Sam. "Just that hedge. Leafy Way is an old-fashioned place. There's an old right of way through the orchard to a back road where there's no gate and no guard at all. Just a chain across the roadway does the trick. This isn't Chicago or Dallas. This is a quiet, law-abiding, country neighborhood. Always has been and always will be."

"Are you sure?" Tash was looking toward the gates where a bored state policeman stood in front of a sentry box, and two lines of people trudged up and down in opposite directions, crossing and re-crossing as if they were performing a figure in a decorous old-fashioned dance.

One line carried signs that read: NO FOOD FOR MURDERING COMMIES!

The other line carried signs that read: DEATH TO CHILD-STARVING FASCISTS!

Sam shifted the heavy camera on his knees and peered through the windshield. "They don't mean any harm. It's just the dock strike. A sort of crossruff. Group One are political exiles from the Caribbean island of Barlovento. They claim the government there is commie and oppose all trade with the island. The local dockworkers' union, strongly anti-Communist since the thirties, is supporting their blockade by going on strike rather than load or unload ships to or from Barlovento. Group Two are Barloventan immigrants, mostly naturalized Americans, living in the barrio, the Spanish-speaking ghetto. They claim the island government is not commie, merely reformist, and the island people will starve next winter unless they can import food and fertilizer from us now."

"How do we get through?"

"Blow your horn and they'll probably let you through."

Tash touched her horn lightly. Both lines fell back. The sentry glanced languidly at the press cards Sam showed him and turned a key in a lock-mechanism that automatically opened the gates.

"That was easy," said Tash. "Perhaps too easy from a security point of view."

"We were expected," said Sam. "It might not have been so easy otherwise."

9

The driveway twisted through a small park of rolling turf and scattered shade trees to a gravel horseshoe in front of a portico with white pillars. The house was brick and stood on a grassy knoll high enough to look over treetops to the roofs of the city beyond.

"Nice view," said Tash. "What do we do now?"

"Ring a doorbell." Sam was climbing out of the car.

"Butler and footmen?"

"You forget this is 1975. They have a chief usher and ushers now, all under civil service and racially integrated."

Tash gave their names to the man who opened the door and they stepped into a hallway, where a wide-flung curve of stair rose like a jet of water from a fountain to the floor above.

On the wall facing the door was a picture painted on silk. Tash recognized a favorite subject of classic Chinese art: *Dragon Playing with a Pearl*. Who but the Chinese would think of a dragon as playful? Who but the Chinese would give a dragon a plaything as tiny and precious as a pearl?

"Must be part of the Governor's private collection," said Sam. "The state couldn't afford anything like that."

"You mean the state has to spend its money on more essential things," retorted Tash.

They followed another usher from hall to corridor to still other corridors until they lost all sense of direction.

"How big is this place?" asked Tash.

"Small compared to the White House," said Sam. "Just forty-two rooms. The indoor staff is only twenty-eight."

The usher threw open a door and announced them:

"Miss Tatiana Perkins, Mr. Samuel Bates."

They walked out of the dim corridor into a blaze of sunshine.

It had once been a terrace. It still had a stone floor, but now it had a slate roof and glass walls like a conservatory.

Beyond the glass was a view of lawn and trees and far-away hills. There were potted plants everywhere: on shelves, on stands, even dangling on chains from the ceiling. Chairs were rattan; cushions, flowered chintz; tables, iron frames topped with glass.

A hearth in the house wall looked as if it had once been an outdoor fireplace, but now it had a mantel of tawny marble. Ferns, growing in earthenware pots, hid the hearthstone.

A canary was singing. His cage was a fantasy of fine wicker twisted into baroque shapes that suggested a Chinese pagoda.

A woman rose.

"I'm Hilary Truance, Mrs. Playfair's social secretary. She will receive you in a moment. Do sit down."

She was a formidable woman, no longer young. Hair in smooth coils the color of polished steel. Eyebrows like the Empress Eugénie in her Winterhalter portraits: thin, arched, permanently raised. Drooping eyelids so she looked out at life through a thicket of sandy lashes. When she was not smiling, her mouth was petulant. Her voice had authority and her clean-cut vowels suggested good schools.

She spoke to Sam. "Will this light do for photos?"

"Perfect." He eased the camera strap off his shoulder and set his camera down on one of the glass-topped tables.

A door opened and an usher's voice said: "Mrs. Playfair."

"I'm so sorry to be late, Hilary." It was a small, breathless voice.

Hilary Truance ignored the apology. "May I present Miss Perkins and Mr. Bates?"

"How do you do? And please sit down. Hilary, I think we would all like some tea."

"Thank you, I'd love it," said Tash.

11

"Me, too. Please," said Sam.

Nothing in Vivian Playfair's photographs had prepared Tash for the dull skin, lifeless hair, and empty eyes. The ghost of a lost beauty lingered only in her felicitous bone structure. She was exquisite but lifeless, like a delicate sea shell when the sea creature has died and dried to mere dust blown along the beach.

Hilary Truance poured the tea, kept the conversation brisk, helped Sam vary the light by raising and lowering Venetian blinds, suggested various poses for Vivian.

When Sam had got all the shots he wanted and they settled down to the interview, Hilary tried to run that, too.

"Are you going to take notes, Miss Perkins?"

"I'd rather tape the interview, if I may."

"You may if you'll send us a transcript to okay before publication."

Tash relished that royal "us."

"Will you give me the okay in writing? That will protect me."

"I suppose so." Hilary's voice was grudging as if she disliked the idea of giving anybody anything.

Tash switched on her tape recorder. It was no bigger than a handbag and ran on batteries.

"Have you any particular topic in mind, Miss Perkins?" demanded Hilary.

"No." Tash deliberately by-passed Hilary. "May I ask if you have any topic in mind, Mrs. Playfair?"

Dutifully, Vivian brought her gaze around to Tash, but the eyes were still empty. "Not really. After all, this interview wasn't my idea."

Tash ventured her first probing question, trying to soften the directness with a gentle voice. "Whose idea was it?"

Hilary intervened at once. "Anyone's. No one's. What

12

could be more obvious than interviewing the Governor's wife? Isn't that what you newspaper people call a 'natural'?"

"This interview is not what this newspaper person would call a natural," returned Tash. "Mrs. Playfair has always refused to be interviewed before, but this time, the suggestion came from the Governor's aide, Mr. de Miranda."

"Oh, no!" Hilary's voice was as steely as her hair. "It was all your editor's idea, not ours."

"Does it really matter?" Vivian Playfair sounded as if she were bored with the whole thing. "What questions would you like to ask me, Miss Perkins?"

"There's one question all newspaper people would like to ask you, if they dared."

"Please dare. What is it?"

Tash took a deep breath. "Is the Governor going to run for a second term this fall?"

Vivian's glance darted to Hilary. Almost imperceptibly, Hilary shook her head.

"I'm sorry." The small voice was colorless. "I can't talk about that."

Poor Bill Brewer! This interview was going to be the usual guff after all.

"Nothing political, if you please, Miss Perkins." Hilary's hard smile was more hostile than any scowl.

Tash was still looking at Vivian. What's the matter with her? Is she sick? Or afraid? She looks at this Hilary Truance the way a retarded child might look at a harsh, psychiatric nurse . . .

For some time Tash had been aware of a sound like the ticking of a loud clock: thock . . . thock . . . thock. Now she identified it, the sound of a tennis ball during a fast rally. She could not see a tennis court through the glass walls, but there must be one somewhere nearby.

13

"Do you like being a Governor's wife, Mrs. Playfair?"

The idiot question got the idiot answer it deserved.

"Who wouldn't? Such a restful life. Nothing to do. Nothing."

Was there a chemical trace of irony there?

Hilary threw herself into the breach once more. "I am sure Miss Perkins' readers would enjoy hearing about your conservation program, Mrs. Playfair."

Vivian looked blank. "What conservation program?"

"Those apple trees." Hilary turned back to Tash. "I'll give you all the documentation before you leave."

Sam looked at Tash quizzically. Had they wasted a whole afternoon getting press releases that would have been mailed to the office anyway?

"Where are these apple trees?" he asked Hilary. "Could I get a shot of them?"

"Come over here and I'll show you."

Sam followed Hilary to a glass door and peered over her shoulder. "Those little things?"

"There are five hundred of them!"

Something plucked at Tash's sleeve. She turned her head. Vivian Playfair was at her elbow, speaking rapidly in a voice just above a whisper.

"Will you do me a great kindness and mail this letter for me when you leave?"

"Why, of course." Tash took the envelope, small, square, white, and dropped it in her handbag.

"Thank you. I really did plant some apple trees here, but I don't think of it as conservation. It was sentiment, really. When I was a little girl I lived in the country and I used to climb an old apple tree in our orchard that I called 'Aunt Apple,' and . . ."

Tash lost the rest.

Two men were coming through the trees side by side, tennis rackets in their hands. Both were tall and lithe and

14

immaculate in tennis white. Sun-light, filtered through leaves above, made the fair head gilt and the dark head black. They moved with the unconscious grace of the young, athletic male, and Tash thought she had never seen a more pleasing sight.

The fair one was the first to see people in the glass-enclosed room. He swerved toward one of the glass doors.

"Governor!" Hilary Truance was taken aback. "I didn't—I thought—"

"Am I intruding?" Jeremy Playfair bent his head below the lintel and stepped into the room.

He was too masculine to be handsome, but there was something engaging about him, an irresistible air of courage and decision.

"This is Tash Perkins," said Vivian. "She's interviewing me. You must have read her column."

Jeremy nodded at Tash as if he scarcely saw her. She was sure he had never heard of her column or of her. His eyes were for his wife only.

"Viv, are you sure you're not overdoing things?"

"Quite sure. I never felt better." She made an effort to match the words with her voice and smile. She almost succeeded. "Miss Perkins, do you know Carlos de Miranda?"

The dark young man bowed to Tash with that shadow of ceremonial flourish inherent in Latin genes. Tash remembered Darwin's account of a French infant, who had never seen French people, but who began to shrug her shoulders before she was a year old. Character might not be inherited, but gesture was.

Vivian finished her story about the apple trees, and Sam went outside to photograph them. Tash tried hard to think of some question that would give a little spice to this blandest of interviews.

15

"Do you think women voters are going to be important in the next election?"

Vivian looked at her husband. "Why don't you answer that one?"

"Of course they're going to be important," said Jeremy. "Women are never going back to a world where their only economic value is their sex."

"Oh!" Tash's eyes were shining. "May I quote you on that?"

"No." Hilary Truance was on her feet.

"Wait a minute, Hilary," protested Jeremy.

But Hilary stood her ground. "Governor, you must not talk as if you liked women."

"Why not? After all, I do."

"But it suggests that women like you. Why else would you like them?"

"And that's bad?"

"Bad? It's political suicide."

"You mean men will see me as a traitor to my sex?"

"I mean men will be jealous. You should make a point of saying something nasty about women every now and then."

"Thank you. I shall make a note of that."

Jeremy and Carlos were both laughing, but Hilary Truance was serious. "Please remember: Being liked by women does not help a male candidate with male voters. It hurts him."

"Don't worry, Hilary," said Carlos. "I'll put a check-rein on his libido until the election is over."

"So you are going to run again?" said Tash.

There was a roar of silence.

"Nothing is decided yet," said the Governor. "And neither I nor Mrs. Playfair have anything to say on that subject for publication."

"I understand." Tash sighed. It would have put her

16

story on the front page if she could have announced the Governor's candidacy. Now she had not got any story and she had annoyed the Governor.

When Sam came back from the apple orchard, Tash rose to take her leave.

"It was an unexpected bonus meeting you," she said to Jeremy Playfair. "I hope some day you'll let me publish your views on women voters."

She smiled at Hilary Truance and Carlos de Miranda, but the smile she gave Vivian Playfair was warmer.

"You've been patient," said Tash. "And generous with your time. Don't worry about your letter. I'll mail it as soon as I get back to town."

"Letter?" The Governor looked quickly at Tash. "What letter?"

"Letter?" repeated Vivian in a cool, steady voice. "I haven't the slightest idea what you're talking about."

3

Tash was late for dinner.

The headwaiter gave her his smile for steady customers and led her to a table by a window with a view of the river.

Gordon Freese struggled to his feet slowly as if he were older than he actually was.

"You're late."

"Sorry." She smiled her thanks to the headwaiter as he pulled out her chair. Like magic, a Campari soda appeared before her. All the waiters here knew her before-dinner drink.

Gordon collapsed rather than sat down.

"Well?" His voice was plaintive.

"I had an extra job today. I had to go to Leafy Way and interview the Governor's wife. I was late getting back."

"I thought you'd given up reporting."

"It was a special assignment."

"You might have telephoned me."

"I didn't have much chance, really. I came here directly from Leafy Way. Only stopped a moment to drop Sam at the office."

"Sam who?"

"Sam Bates, the photographer who went with me."

Tash looked across the table and wondered for the hundredth time: How did I ever allow myself to drift into a relationship like this?

The most logical answer was the most humiliating: Gordon was the only game in town.

Tash was a realist. At twenty-five, she knew she had missed the young mating season. Most of the men she met now would be the proverbially very married or very promiscuous or very homosexual. Gordon was the only one she had met who had seemed to her truly uncommitted, as if he might be a male version of herself: lonely and a little shy about love-making.

Now it was beginning to dawn on her that, in addition to the married, the promiscuous, and the homosexual, there might be a fourth category: the neuter.

Ethologists had found individuals among birds and mammals in nature who abstained from courtship during the breeding season, though dissection did not reveal any anatomical difference between them and the others. Did something like that explain Gordon?

If love is "egoism for two," her dalliance with Gordon was loneliness for two.

Suddenly, tonight, it seemed intolerable.

Why tonight?

Had it anything to do with that vision of two young men in tennis white, sauntering under trees, their heads dappled with sunlight?

How entirely different this evening would be if either Carlos de Miranda or Jeremy Playfair were sitting on the other side of the table.

Perhaps it was better to stay at home with a good book or a bad television show, than to go out in the evening with the Gordons of this world.

"I am hesitating between sweetbreads *financière* or duck *à l'orange*," announced Gordon.

He was one of those people who can consume a vast amount of calories without gaining an ounce. She had scarcely noticed this before. Tonight, like everything else about him, it irritated her.

"I'll have lamb chops and string beans, please."

"Dieting again?"

"I have to, now I spend more time sitting a typewriter than riding or playing tennis."

"I sit at a desk all day, but I do not have to diet."

"Congratulations."

"You are in a frightfully negative mood tonight."

"Sorry."

"What is the matter?"

"I don't know."

But she did know. She could have answered his question in one word: you.

Was it his job that made him what he was? Or had he sought the job because he was born that way? He was a civil servant hidden away in an arcane niche of the labyrinthine Department of Progress and Rehabilitation in nearby Washington. His job was his favorite subject of conversation.

". . . and so I told him that eight copies are always made of every *aide-mémoire* in our section and one of those eight should always come to my desk as a matter of routine. He couldn't answer that. He didn't even try. So now I am biding my time. If I do not find a copy of the next *aide-mémoire* on my desk the day it is sent out, I shall take the law into my own hands and go over his head to the Deputy Assistant Secretary. It is a revolutionary thing to do, but what else can I do when a matter of principle is at stake? And—Tash! You're not listening!"

"Oh, yes, I am. What happens to all these *aides-mémoires* in a year or so?"

"They are stored in a warehouse."

"How long has your section been making eight copies of everything?"

"Since World War Two."

"Must be a pretty big warehouse."

She had hoped for a smile, but he answered seriously: "It is. Very big."

Suddenly, she was thankful things had never gone further between them. He would be a sober, industrious lover. He would read all the sex manuals about "arousing" a woman and bring to love-making the same patience and calculation that he would bring to the coupling of two engines. It would not occur to him that to be joyous such things must be spontaneous and mutual as they are in nature.

Rain was falling when they reached the parking lot after dinner.

Tash looked across the open space to a shopping center where neon lights advertised a liquor store.

"I haven't a drop of anything to drink. Let's pick up something over there."

"You needn't bother for my sake," said Gordon. "I'm just as happy without it."

"Then I'll bother for my sake," said Tash. "I'm not just as happy without it."

Gordon cast one longing look at his dry, warm car, then turned up his coat collar and plodded after her through the drizzle.

It was a self-service place, more like a supermarket than an old-fashioned wine merchant's. Shelves along four aisles displayed row upon row of glittering bottles, each ticketed with its price.

Gordon stopped at the cashier's desk to buy cigarettes, while Tash wandered down the first aisle looking for a bottle of Madeira, her favorite after-dinner drink.

21

"Please, ma'am, can y'all tell me if this here is the cheapest sherry wine?"

It was the soft speech of the rural, western counties.

She turned her head and saw at her right elbow a frail boy with hair like thistledown floating around a delicate face. Pale eyes, half-closed, blurred, blind-looking. An elfin smile. He might have been a fallen angel who could still remember Paradise.

"Aren't you a little young to be buying wine?"

"I'm older than I look."

"These California sherries are the cheapest. This one is sweet and this one dry. Less sweet."

"Thank ya, ma'am." He didn't even bother to look at the sherry. He was edging away.

"These are from New York state, and—"

"Yeah. Thanks."

He was still edging away. Didn't he want to buy? Was the price too steep?

She reached for a bottle of rainwater Madeira and turned to drop it in the wire basket on her left arm. Her handbag, dangling by its strap from the same arm, was wide open. The pocket inside, where she kept her wallet, was empty.

She looked up and saw a tall man. He had a cast in one eye and a mouth that twisted down at one corner. He was holding her wallet in one hand. In the other he was holding a white envelope.

She reached for the wallet, crying out: "That's mine!"

With one blow, he knocked her to the floor.

Anger brought her to her feet. No one else was near her. No one else was looking toward her. But she could see the backs of of the tall man and the angelic boy moving away from her down the aisle toward the door. They were not running, but neither were they loitering. And they were together.

"Stop! Wait a minute!"

Heads turned to look at her as she ran after them.

They were passing the cashier's desk when they heard her cry.

They broke into a run.

"Gordon! Stop them! They've got my wallet."

Gordon stood and stared at them, mouth open. Another man, coming through the revolving door, heard her and tried to block their way. He was flung side as they pushed through the door.

Tash followed them.

There was a crowd of after-dinner shoppers in the parking lot, but no sign of the man or the boy. Either they had melted into the crowd or hidden in the darkness beyond the lighted windows.

A police car was parked at the curb with two men in it.

"My wallet." Tash was panting now. "They took it. A man and a boy. They just came out of the liquor store. Didn't you see them?"

The policeman near the curb shook his head. "Which way did they go, lady?"

"I don't know. When I got outside, there was no sign of them."

"You followed them? They might have broken your arm or worse."

"I know. It was stupid. But I just wasn't thinking. I didn't have time to think."

"You were lucky they got away. Were there witnesses?"

"The people in the store."

"Then I'd better talk to them. Wait here, Joe."

Inside the store, a dozen or so customers were gathered around the cashier's desk, all talking at once.

"Officer, the man was short and blond and young."

"No, he was well over six feet and swarthy and built like a football player."

"There were two men," said Gordon. "And one had a knife. That's why I didn't try to stop them."

"I didn't see no knife!"

The policeman looked at Tash. "You see? We'll never get a description."

"Why don't you ask me for one?" she retorted. "I'm the only person who had a close look at them. There were two, a man and a boy. The boy distracted me while the man took my wallet out of my bag."

"Sounds like a pro caper," said the policeman. "You'd better come to the precinct station house tomorrow and see if you can identify them from mug shots. What's your name and address?"

She told him.

"What does the wallet look like?"

"Brown. Real alligator. I got it before I knew alligators were an endangered species." She realized she was babbling and tried to pull herself together. "It was lined with tan calfskin. Flat and thin. More like a billfold than a wallet."

"Do you know how much money was in it?"

"Thirty-nine dollars."

The policeman was writing all this down in his notebook slowly and laboriously. Tash had an impression he would be handier with a nightstick than a pen.

"Was there anything else in the wallet besides cash?"

"No . . . Yes, there was. I almost forgot. A blank check for emergencies. And an identification card. It came with the wallet. I filled it in long ago. Name, address, and telephone number."

"You mean you signed this identification card?"

"Yes, I did."

"In ink?"

She nodded.

"Then you'd better notify your bank the first thing tomorrow morning."

"Why?"

"They've got a blank check of yours and a signature of yours to copy. Quite a temptation to forgery."

He closed his notebook. He had turned toward the door when a second thought struck him. He turned back to Tash again.

"Did they take anything else besides the wallet?"

"I don't think so."

"Better check."

She emptied the contents of her bag on the counter beside the cashier's desk. Credit cards, driver's license, car registration, press card, keys, pen, address book, coin purse, tissues . . .

"I have a feeling something's missing," she said. "But I just can't think what it is."

"You may think of it by tomorrow. If you do, you can tell them at the station house."

Now the policeman was gone, everyone gathered around Tash. Did she know there was a cut on her cheekbone? The man who struck her must have worn a ring. The cashier reached under the counter, brought out a first aid kit, put iodine and a BandAid on the cheek bone. Did she need money for bus fare home?

Gordon stepped into the circle. "I'm driving her home."

"What about my car?" said Tash.

"Leave it here for tonight."

It was a relief to get away from the crowd with its open sympathy and curiosity and its furtive delight in shock and sensation.

She wondered how long her hands had been shaky and her knees rubbery. She had not noticed either until now.

She drew in a deep breath of the outdoor air, cold enough to feel fresh even though it was loaded with carbon monoxide.

Gordon swerved toward his own car. Tash halted. "Just a minute, please. There's something I must get out of my car first. My tape of the interview with Vivian Playfair. It was too bulky for my handbag, so I put it in the glove compartment . . . Here it is, but . . ."

Her voice faded into silence.

"What's wrong?"

"Gordon, I've remembered. The other thing they took besides my wallet. It was a letter Mrs. Playfair asked me to mail for her. I put it in my bag."

"You're sure it's missing?"

"Not only that. I saw it in the man's hand. A square, white envelope."

"Funny they'd take a letter instead of your credit cards," said Gordon.

"Very funny." But Tash did not laugh.

"Are you frightened?"

"I believe I am. Now."

"Why?"

"That blank check they took had my name and address printed on it. I wish they didn't know who I am and where I live."

4

THERE ARE 12.1 million people in the United States who live alone. Tash was one of them.

She was lucky enough to have the top floor of a house on Water Street, the oldest part of town, where artists and writers now flocked so they could have a river view.

Her attic floor had once been servants' quarters. Now the landlord had knocked down partitions, cut one large, modern window in the wall overlooking the river, installed a small kitchen and a smaller bathroom, and called the whole thing a studio.

After weighing the disadvantages of climbing five flights of stairs against the advantages of a high view, he had generously decided not to charge any more rent for the studio than he did for large apartments on the first and second floors.

Tash kept her typewriter on the dining table and the dining table by the big window, so she could have the view and room to spread out her papers at the same time.

This morning her eyes kept wandering from the keyboard to the gulls that flew above the river. Why was it so hard for her to write this silly story about Vivian Playfair?

Thank heaven there was no rush about a feature story

of this sort. Bill would probably hold it over for the Sunday magazine if he thought it worth printing at all, with the Governor insisting that the only interesting bits must be left out. Who wanted to read about apple trees, even if there were five hundred of them?

Toward noon Tash gathered up the pages she had typed and put them in a manila envelope. The tape of the interview went into the pocket of her suit jacket. She put a topcoat over the jacket and and buttoned it up to her chin. No pickpocket was going to get that tape. She had a feeling she should hang on to the only proof there was that Vivian Playfair had given her a letter to mail.

Fortunately, it was one of those sunny, windy April mornings that feel colder than they look. She was glad of the topcoat as she leaned against a solid wall of wind, walking around the corner to the police precinct station house.

It was a new building, its outside planned by an architect who had allowed his fancy to dwell a little too long on Karnak and Babylon. Inside, he had throttled fancy down to something halfway between clinic and jail.

A uniformed man directed her to the detective bureau on the third floor. The door was open. As she drew near she heard three male voices earnestly discussing the baseball season.

She paused in the doorway. Two men were in mufti, one in uniform. They must have seen her standing in the doorway, yet they went on talking as if she wasn't there, until the telephone rang.

The man in uniform reached for it.

"Yeah? Yeah! Yeah . . ."

He turned to the others. "Got to get along now."

After he had passed Tash in the doorway, one of the men in mufti looked at her sternly as though she had kept him waiting.

28

"Well? What do you want?"

The moment she gave her name and the address of the newspaper, he remembered the case and his manner changed.

"Could you describe these two guys, ma'am?"

"One was tall and gaunt. Middle-aged. With a cast in one eye. The other was a boy, hardly more than a child. Light hair. Angelic face. Eyes that were not so angelic. They wore T-shirts, black leather jackets, jeans, and sneakers. No hats or caps."

Her detective glanced across the room at the other detective.

"Sound familiar?"

"Sure does. Halcón and one of his *polluelitos.*"

"Al Cone?" said Tash.

"No, Halcón. The H is silent. It's Spanish for hawk. He's a Barlo."

"You mean a Barloventan?"

"That's right."

"What else is he?"

"Just a guy we've known a long time."

"And what are his *polluelitos?*"

That question seemed to embarrass the policeman. "His chicks. Kids who work for him. He's what they call a chicken hawk. The kid you describe sounds like one they call Freaky."

"Why Freaky?"

"He has some rather freakish pastimes. We don't have a mug-shot of him, but—Hang on a minute."

He went to a filing cabinet and came back with a manila envelope that contained several papers. He riffled through them, picked out one, and flicked it across the desk to Tash. "That him?"

She looked down at photographs attached to the same sheet of cardboard, one full face, one profile, the same number stenciled on each.

The profile was no use to her, but the full face showed a cast in one eye and a down-turned mouth that were unmistakable. There had been another face something like that in Scottish history, the face of "gleyed Argyle." Behind that other crooked mask there had been a highly intelligent mind and a formidable will to power.

"I think that's the man," said Tash. "Though I only saw him for a few seconds."

"You were lucky to see him at all. He didn't expect that. He had the chick there to distract you, so you wouldn't. If we can arrest him, will you identify him as the man you saw with your wallet in his hand?"

"I'd have to."

"Why does that bother you?"

"I suppose because it puts so much responsibility on me. It would be so awful if I made a mistake."

The detective's sigh was purposely loud so Tash could hear it.

"People like you are always griping about crime in the streets. Then, when it strikes, you hesitate to testify—if you're still alive. There was another case like yours last night. Purse-snatcher knocked a girl down and her head hit the curbstone. She died of a skull fracture in the hospital this morning. That could have happened to you."

"I realize that."

"Do you? I wonder. Ever seen anyone lying in the street dead?"

Tash had to admit she hadn't.

"Was anything else taken besides your wallet?"

She opened her lips to say: *Yes, there was a letter.*

How could she drag the Governor's wife into the police investigation of a petty crime? Especially when the Governor's wife had already denied that such a letter ever existed?

30

She shook her head.

The detective was studying the Band-Aid on her forehead. "Cut all right now?"

"It's healing."

"Any other injuries?"

"A few bruises from falling."

"If he'd really beaten you up, we would have refunded the thirty-nine dollars you lost. State law. As it is, you can probably take it as a loss on your income tax return. Ask your accountant."

As Tash went down the corridor, a male voice floated after her from the still open doorway: "Now, as I was saying about the Orioles . . ."

She took a taxi to the parking lot where she had left her car last night and then drove to the bank. There she found another established routine that made crime seem commonplace, almost cosy and domesticated.

"That missing blank check is nothing to worry about. Just go through your check book and write the initial letter of your surname in front of the serial number on each check. Then, if a check of yours should come through without that letter, we'll know at once that it's a forgery, and we'll notify the police."

By the time she got to the newspaper office, she was feeling that mixture of relief and recovery that we call convalescence.

Bill Brewer threw down a ball-point pen and pushed a lock of hair out of his eyes.

"Glad to see you're all in one piece."

"What did you expect?"

"The AP story last night said you'd been knocked down with bruises and contusions—whatever contusions are. I called the police, and they said you were okay, so I didn't call you. Sleep well?"

"Like a top." She took her typescript out of its en-

31

velope and laid it on the desk. "There's the Playfair story, the printable part." She pulled the roll of tape out of her pocket. "And there's the part we can't print."

"What on earth . . .?"

"I suggest you read the script first."

He glanced through it and sighed. "Pretty bland. Tape any better?"

"Oh, yes."

"Why can't we use it?"

"If you listen to it, you'll understand."

"Put it on my machine."

Once more Bill assumed his favorite listening posture, leaning back in his swivel chair, hands clasped behind his neck, eyes half-closed.

Vivian Playfair's voice came through—clear, colorless, child-like: *Will you do me a great kindness and mail this letter for me when you leave?*

And Tash's own answer: *Why, of course.*

"Don't they have mail collection at Leafy Way?" said Bill.

"Wait," said Tash. "More coming."

Suddenly Bill sat up. "I'll be damned! He is going to run for a second term."

"But we can't quote him. There's something else coming in a minute. Listen."

Again, it was Vivian's voice, clear in the silence: *Letter? I haven't the slightest idea what you're talking about.*

As the sound ended, the tape cut loose from its moorings and flapped like a pennant in the breeze.

Bill shut off the machine.

"I suppose she thought your microphone was not sensitive enough to pick up her whisper."

"It wasn't a whisper," said Tash. "It was the next tone just above a whisper."

"Suggesting she knows the sibilance of a whisper can

32

attract as much attention as a shout in a quiet room."

"Don't most people know that?"

"Only people with some experience of intrigue."

"I haven't told anyone else. Was that right?"

"Right and necessary. Even though you've got the tape to prove it happened, we won't use the story for two reasons. Betraying a confidence never does a newspaper any good in the long run, and we are supporting Playfair's candidacy. We don't want to hurt him through her or any other way. Who was the letter addressed to? Or didn't you notice?"

"I didn't really notice, but one thing happened to catch my eye. It was addressed to a Dr.—not a Mr. or Mrs. or Ms."

"When did you mail it?"

"I didn't have time to mail it before the pickpocket took it."

"What?"

"Didn't I tell you that the pickpocket took it?"

"No, you did not. Did you tell the police that?"

"No, I didn't. You see, I liked Mrs. Playfair, and I was afraid of getting her into trouble. Of course it must be just coincidence that a pickpocket should take something I had belonging to someone else."

"Coincidence?" Bill repeated the word as if it were unfamiliar. "I wonder."

"You can't think my pocket was picked just to get Vivian Playfair's letter? And that my wallet was stolen just to make me think it was an ordinary theft?"

"Why not?"

"Bill, are you serious?"

"Some people are surprised at the amount of scandal that gets into newspapers. I'm always surprised at the amount of scandal that doesn't get into newspapers. For every story we print, there are a dozen we can't or won't print. I think this is one of them. So let's send this silly script over to Leafy Way by messenger for Mrs. Play-fair's okay and use it in the Sunday magazine and forget everything else about it."

When Tash went to bed that night, she did not get to sleep for a long time. False dawn was leaching darkness out of the sky when her eyes finally closed.

The telephone woke her.

She opened her eyes to bright sunshine and a blue sky. The hands of the clock pointed to twelve noon.

She rolled over to the edge of the bed and scooped the telephone from the bedside table.

This would be Bill Brewer asking if she had any idea how much longer they would have to wait for an okay on the Playfair story.

"Hello?"

"Miss Perkins?" She could not place the resonant, baritone voice at once, but it identified itself quickly. "This is Carlos de Miranda."

"Oh . . ."

"The Governor is pleased with your treatment of the interview with Mrs. Playfair. So is she."

"I'm glad. Are there any changes?"

"No, it can be printed as it is, but . . . something else has come up. The Governor would like to see you. He would be most grateful if you could come out to Leafy Way again this afternoon. Is that possible?"

"Why, yes. Of course."

"Would three o'clock be convenient?"

"Yes, but can't you give me some idea what this is all about?"

The moment's hesitation was almost imperceptible.

"Perhaps I should. Then you will have a little time to think things over before you come. The Governor's chief

34

speech writer is ill. If the Governor decides to run for a second term, he must get someone else at once. I've been reading your political columns for months. I suggested that you might be able to get a leave of absence from your paper and take on the job. Are you interested?"

"I'm overwhelmed, but I'll have to think it over."

"Why don't you talk it over with your editor, Mr. Brewer, now, and then come to see us at three o'clock?"

"I'll do that if Bill Brewer's available. And thank you."

"It is we who shall be in your debt."

Most North Americans sound a little foolish talking with old-fashioned ceremony, but the same words spoken with a trace of Spanish accent do not sound foolish at all. Carlos de Miranda would have sounded foolish if he had tried to ape North America's slang and spurious intimacy between strangers.

Half an hour later Tash was in Bill's office.

"Miranda called me after he talked to you," said Bill. "He wants me to urge you to take the job."

"Are you going to?"

"It's your decision, Tash. You do realize you'll be taking a pay cut? The State can never pay you as much as newspaper syndication."

"I know that." Tash smiled. "This job offer is not a bribe."

"No," said Bill. "It's true the Governor has just lost a speech writer and is looking for a new one. I checked that with our political reporters."

"So you think that the offer may be just what it seems? That I was chosen solely on the basis of my political columns?"

"And also perhaps on the basis of your visit to Leafy Way. Perhaps you weren't interviewing Mrs. Playfair.

35

Perhaps Playfair was interviewing you. Perhaps he wanted to see the kind of person you were before he offered you this job. That would explain why Mrs. Playfair, who never gives interviews, suddenly decided to give one, though she really had nothing to say."

"You're assuming she then took advantage of a situation the Governor had created to sneak a letter out of the house through me?"

"That would explain her being a few minutes late for the interview rather neatly. She stopped on her way to the Florida Room to scribble a note when she wasn't under the eye of Hilary Truance."

"But why would the Governor's wife have to sneak anything?"

"When you live in a goldfish bowl there can be all sorts of innocent reasons for something like that. Privacy is like sleep—something you don't appreciate until you have to go without it."

"So you've gone back to the idea that it was just bad luck the letter was intercepted by a pickpocket?"

"It looks that way now. To think otherwise is to invent an explanation too elaborate for your needs, a practise abhorred by all good scientists. . . . Do you want to take this job, Tash?"

"I think I do."

"Why? To be inside history? To be where power is? To watch decisions made?"

"No."

"Then why? You must have some reason."

"No reason. Just a feeling that this is something I have to do."

"We're going to miss you."

"Bill, if you really need me here, I'll turn it down."

Bill smiled. "Dear Tash, I think we may be able to struggle along without you for a few months, but remember: you can always come back here if anything goes wrong."

It was Tash's turn to smile. "What could possibly go wrong?"

5

THE GOVERNOR'S HOUSE at Leafy Way was shaped like an E.

The front was a classic oblong. At the sides two long wings extended toward the back, framing a courtyard. The Florida Room formed the short, center bar of the E between the two wings.

The far end of the West Wing housed kitchen and pantries and laundries. The far end of the East Wing housed executive offices, where worker bees toiled anonymously for the good of the hive; secretaries, file clerks, researchers, and speech writers.

That next morning, when a page conducted Tash to her new office, the first thing she saw on her desk was a morning edition of her own newspaper.

GROW YOUR OWN APPLES
SAYS MRS. PLAYFAIR
by Tash Perkins

Months ago she and Bill Brewer had worried about whether it should be Tatiana or Tash. She didn't like nicknames used as full names, but Bill had said Tatiana was too foreign. Now it didn't seem to matter. It would be a long time before that by-line appeared in print again.

A tap on the door.

"Come in!"

Carlos de Miranda walked into the room carrying some books.

"Welcome to Leafy Way!"

He sounded manorial, as if he had been welcoming guests to official residences for years. Perhaps he had . . .

"First of all, I must tell you about the alarm system for your office," he announced.

"Does each room here have its own alarm system?"

"Only each office. In the rest of the house, each suite of rooms has its own system, and each floor has its own fuse box in the hall. Like all the others, your alarm is a combined burglar and fire alarm. You know it's on when this red button is lighted. There are push buttons inside and outside your office, so you can turn it on or off, whether you are in the office or not."

"You can't mean that anyone outside can turn it off in order to break in!"

"Oh, no! Only you can turn it on, or off, outside or inside, because it works on a numerical combination that only you know. It has to be a number of five digits, and you can change it as often as you like."

Tash laughed. "I'll be sure to forget the number and lock myself out."

"So would I without something to remember it by. I use the digits for my birthday date. That's a number I can't forget."

"I'll do the same. My birthday is March 29, 1950."

Carlos pushed the numbered buttons for her: 29–3–50.

"You've done it wrong!" cried Tash. "It'll have to be 3–29–50, if I'm to remember it, because that's the way I think of numerical dates."

"A month-day-year sequence? Okay." He corrected the number and put the books he was carrying on the table. "Have you everything you want in here?"

Tash smiled. "Everything. Typewriter, tape recorder, papers, pens, pencils, even comfortable chairs and a nice view of flower beds. Everything but work."

"Don't worry. There will be more than enough of that, I assure you."

He sat on the edge of a window seat and held out a cigarette case.

"No, thanks. I gave it up two years ago, but it doesn't bother me when other people smoke."

"What strength of character! Some day I am going to be virtuous, too, but now, like Saint Augustine, I am asking God to wait until I am a little older." He drew on his own cigarette luxuriously. "Do you read Spanish?"

"Only a little."

"Then it's just as well most of these books are in English." He took an ashtray from the table and set it on his lap. "What do you know about Barlovento?"

"Nothing."

"Fine. Then you won't have anything to unlearn. I was born there, but educated in America. I was a classmate of the Governor's at Princeton. I'm an American now, but . . . how can I be indifferent to the fate of Barlovento when it is becoming a football in American politics?"

"The dock strike?"

He nodded. "Barlovento is mining country. America needs bauxite from those mines, but the dockworkers' union had such a bad experience with Communist infiltration during the thirties that they won't unload any imports from Barlovento, which, they say, is Communist."

"Is it?"

40

Carlos shrugged with Latin elaboration. "Such polarized terms have little meaning in an economy as primitive as Barlovento's. The dictator, Escudero, calls himself an agrarian reformer. He has trade relations with Russia, like everybody else today, including us. If he is handled with tact, he is more likely to evolve into a Tito than a Mao. His predecessor, the neo-fascist Roya, was far worse. The Mafia ruled Barlovento through Roya. Indeed, it was to escape Roya that my father brought his family to this country."

"And where do I come in?"

"There are two factions among Barlovantan-Americans now: immigrants, who are pro-Escudero and want the Governor to break the strike, and political exiles, who are anti-Escudero and want the Governor to support the strike.

"One thing that confuses people is the fact that the anti-strike faction is liberal and the pro-strike faction is conservative.

"In a few days the Governor will have to make a speech about all this. You are going to write the speech."

"Which side do I take?"

"Can you ask? Neither, of course! He must say nothing in a great many words and so buy time for negotiation. This is what I believe speech writers call a challenge."

"But won't he have to take sides eventually?"

"If he's lucky, the President will step in and stop the strike as a matter of national interest. Then the Governor won't be compromised. That's important to him because this is an election year."

"So he is going to run for a second term?"

"Of course. That was decided months ago." Carlos smiled. "Now you're one of us, we don't have to pretend with you any more."

"Anything else?"

41

"Just remember to walk on eggs whenever you mention the Barloventan crisis."

"In other words, dodge it?"

"Exactly."

Tash remembered her first day as a reporter. She had covered a story about the sale of a Fragonard drawing for a fabulous sum. When there wasn't time to look up the date of the drawing before going to press, she had asked the city editor what to do about it. He had answered, without looking up from his work: "Dodge it!"

To a girl fresh from academia where accuracy and honesty were gods, it had been a shock. Now she was getting used to this other world, where the only goal was getting things done, however sloppily or deviously.

"How did you learn so much about American newspapers?" she asked Carlos.

"Not so long ago I was running the South American department in the New York office of a North American wire service. When Jeremy found out how many Barloventan-American voters there were in this state, he decided he needed a press aide who could talk to them in their own tongue. So here I am!"

"Barlovento means windward, doesn't it?"

"So you do know some Spanish?"

"Not as much as I'd like to."

"In that part of the Caribbean, the prevailing wind is such that it was always easier for Spain to invade leeward islands, like Sotavento, in sailing ships than windward islands, like Barlovento. So Barlovento got its freedom long before Sotavento and was always more free until Roya took over. Why not put that in the speech? Say something about the gallantry of the liberty-loving Barloventistos, who threw off the iron yoke of tyrannical Spain over one hundred years ago, etcetera. Revolutions as old as that are respectable. The safest way to give *brio* to a newspaper story is by whipping a dead horse, and—"

He paused at the sound of staccato footsteps outside in the corridor.

The door burst open, and an angry, little man plunged into the room.

"Carlos! Why are you hiding back here?"

"I am not hiding. I am explaining to Miss Perkins—"

"*Miss* Perkins?" The little man turned to stare at Tash. "Well, I'll be jiggered! I always thought Tash Perkins was a man. The name sounds like a man's and the columns read like a man's."

Tash was nettled. "Would you say Lise Meitner's equations and formulae read like a man's?"

Carlos interrupted in his most formal tone: "Miss Perkins, may I present the Lieutenant Governor, Mr. Job Jackman?"

In the neighboring state of Maryland, there was no lieutenant governor, but here he was an important officer, presiding over the Senate and performing all functions of a national vice president at state level.

The gap between the dignity of the office and the personality of this small, uninhibited man was enormous. Beside Job, Carlos was like a large, calm, splendid Saint Bernard dog, while Job himself seemed like a yapping, feisty, little terrier.

"I'll call you Tash. You call me Job. Everybody does. Is that your car outside? The blue convertible? It's rolled. I came in to tell you."

"Oh, no!"

"Oh, yes! Come on out and look."

It hadn't rolled far. A tree had stopped it, denting one of the front fenders.

"This is the second time it's happened this month!" wailed Tash.

"It's that automatic drive," said Job. "So easy when you're in a hurry to put the gear indicator on *N* for neutral instead of *P* for park. You do it by sight, not by feel, the way you did the old gear shifts, and sight can be deceptive."

"I'll watch it in future," said Tash.

"You'd better." Job took a cigar from his pocket and made a business of lighting it. Once he had it going, he went on in the same rapid-fire style. "Has Carlos been loading you to the eyebrows with stuff about Barlovento?"

Carlos opened his mouth, but Job stifled his protest with a raised hand. "Forget it!" Job went on. "Who cares one good goddamn about what happens to Barlovento?"

"Now wait a minute!" cried Carlos. "There is a large Barloventan vote in this country, and if you took the trouble to read history—"

"You told me yourself this morning that there are no good histories of Barlovento in English," retorted Job. "And you know that I don't know one word of Spanish. But I do know that all the voters in this state really care about is the gut issues. What I'd like to see in the Governor's next speech is a pledge to stop inflation, lower taxes, and raise food prices."

"You're joking," said Tash.

"I never joke about politics."

"But you said *raise* food prices!"

"Of course I did. There are only two industrial counties in this state. The other seventeen are all farming counties. Seventeen counties are a lot of voters, and they all want food prices to go up."

Carlos burst out laughing. "My dear Miss Perkins, do not let our Mr. Jackman intimidate you with his impersonation of Boss Tweed. Neither he nor I decide policy around here. Only the Governor himself, and he will talk to you about all this at luncheon. Oh, didn't I mention that you're lunching with him today? Drinks in the Florida Room at one o'clock. Come on, Job. Miss Perkins has work to do."

At five minutes to one Tash stepped through the door that led from the executive offices to the rest of the house.

The first thing she heard was a bird singing.

She followed the sound and it led her to the Florida Room, where Vivian Playfair's canary was pouring out his heart in a fountain of song.

Vivian herself stood by the cage, listening.

One look at her and Tash was speechless.

This was another woman from the woman who had received her last Monday.

It was not just the change in clothes, though that was part of it. She had taken trouble with what she wore this time. Her raw-silk slacks and short-sleeved cashmere sweater were the yellow of the canary's plumage, a streak of sunshine in a room now dimmer with the Venetian blinds drawn. Their cut revealed a Tanagra figure—wasp waist, small, high bosom, gently rounded hipline, long legs. But the real change was in the woman herself.

This time she looked young for her twenty-eight years. Her eyes were a clean, bright blue. Her hair, loosely shaped to frame her face, had a pale gloss with golden highlights. Her skin seemed to glow softly like light shining through alabaster. With all the yellow, she was wearing coral beads and a coral ring, the pink shade of coral that has yellow in its composition.

This was the legendary Vivian Playfair whose looks and taste had provided so much copy for Sunday newspapers and women's magazines.

45

"Miss Perkins, I am so glad you are going to work with us for a while. I liked the interview and so did Jerry."

It took Tash a moment to realize that "Jerry" meant Jeremy.

"We were both distressed when we read in the papers that your pocket had been picked after you left here. Did you lose much?"

"Only thirty-nine dollars and that letter you—"

Vivian interrupted gently. "Did Hilary Truance assign you a room of your own here?"

"An office? Yes, when I got here this morning, a page—"

"You'll need more than an office when the campaign gets under way. You've no idea of the organized frenzy that goes on during an election. There'll be nights when you work too late to go home afterward, so you'll have to have a place here where you can flop for a few hours. Tell Hilary I said so. I think there's a suite of rooms near hers, but if not, she'll find you something elsewhere."

"Thank you. About that letter—"

"Carlos!" Vivian's glance went beyond Tash to the doorway. Her smile was radiant as she held out her hand. Carlos bowed his head to brush her fingers with his lips. He turned to Tash without losing a beat and smiled.

"I meant to show you the way here, but I see you didn't need me."

"I followed the canary's song," said Tash.

"Ah, Blondel!" Carlos went over to the cage. The bird seemed to know him well for it did not flutter. "You are no longer a minstrel," he whispered, lips close to the bars. "You are merely a luncheon bell."

"I am dying for a martini," said Vivian. "And I imagine that Miss Perkins is, too."

"Don't I see sherry?" said Tash.

"You do indeed." Carlos moved to the drinks table. "The best of all pre-luncheon drinks, as anyone with a drop of Spanish blood will tell you. This I ordered myself."

The moment Tash tasted it, she knew it was special. She sipped it slowly, so she was still savoring it when Hilary Truance came into the room.

"Martini?" inquired Carlos.

"Need you ask?" Her roving glance fell on Tash. "So you're one of us now. Welcome to the madhouse!"

"It seems a well-regulated madhouse."

"Wait till the campaign starts."

Vivian crossed the room to them. "Hilary, she will need a room for overnight."

"All set. She's to have the suite next to mine."

"Mrs. Playfair," said Tash. "If I may, I would like to explain about that letter."

"Not now, if you please, Miss Perkins. Some other time."

Tash was not used to flat rejection or a voice of ice. Why should Mrs. Playfair treat her as an enemy? What could be more natural than wanting to explain what had happened to a letter she had been trusted to mail?

Hilary was looking at Tash over the rim of her cocktail glass. "There are a lot of things I'll have to explain to you. Maybe after luncheon. Damn this election! There's no time for anything else. I can't even work on my book."

"What's your book about?"

"The structure of society. After all, I am a social secretary." Her laugh was as harsh as the grinding of gears. "It's called *In Defense of Snobbery.*"

Tash blinked. "I gather you don't agree that the word snob comes from *sine nobilitas*—without nobility?"

"I don't care whether it does or not. I decided to write this book when I heard someone say that good grammar is snobbish, and—"

47

But Tash was no longer listening. The Governor had just come into the room.

Job Jackman was with him, and a small, plump woman, who was introduced as Mrs. Jackman and addressed by the others as Jo Beth.

Everyone present now was a memeber of Jeremy Playfair's famous "Tennis Cabinet," a close-knit group that worked and played with him: his own wife, the Jackmans, Mrs. Truance, and Miranda. The only one missing was Captain Wilkes, who commanded the state police guard at Leafy Way.

They moved to the adjoining breakfast room, where luncheon was usually served, as well as breakfast.

Tash discovered from a place card that she was on the Governor's left. He was polite and even cordial to Tash when he remembered she was there, but most of the time his eyes were on his wife at the other end of the table. Once when he was speaking to Tash he said, "Miss ...er..." and she had to supply the Perkins. She thought then: There will never be anything very personal about this relationship, and turned to the woman on her left.

Jo Beth Jackman was just about what one would expect Job's wife to be: simple, serious, dressed carefully rather than smartly. She looked just about Job's age, and Tash put them down as old high school sweethearts.

Jo Beth talked about her two sons, both in college, and showed their pictures to Tash. They looked like the kind of boys Tash would like to have herself some day.

"I miss them," Jo Beth sighed. "I miss the life we used to live at our ranch out West. We've rented a sort of country place here, Fox Run, but it's too suburban. The boys don't like to spend their vacations there. They miss the horses and mountain trails and all that. So do I. I'm just not cut out for this sort of life."

"I don't suppose anybody is."

"They are." Jo Beth looked at Jeremy and then down the table at Vivian. "They are both perfect in their parts, and I think the Governor enjoys every minute of it. Sometimes I wonder about Vivian. She doesn't take the slightest interest in social questions that interest Jeremy, yet, personally, she is compassionate. Her maid, Juana Fernandez, is a Barloventan immigrant who couldn't get a job with anyone else. Total illiteracy and no English."

"But Mrs. Playfair took her on?"

"Yes. I met Juana through settlement work. I told Vivian about her, and Vivian promptly offered her this job as personal maid to tide her over until she could learn English and go on to a better job. Few women would have done that.

"Why not?"

"Oh, I didn't tell you? Juana's face is monstrously scarred, the result of being questioned by secret police under the Roya regime. That face is a much greater handicap than lack of English or illiteracy. Employers, both men and women, took one look at it and said, 'No.' It was something they did not want to look at every day. Yet Vivian accepted it as part of her daily life. There is more to Vivian than most people think."

Over coffee, the Governor got down to business with Tash.

"Let me give you a quick run-down on my personal prejudices in writing and speaking.

"I like everything short—speeches, paragraphs, sentences, and words. I like a frequent change of pace. Monotony will put any audience to sleep. I don't like starting with a corny joke. Plunge *in medias res* like Horace.

"I like salt and pepper; wit, not clowning. Some people object that wit hurts. That's why we should use it. Politics is a fight. The word 'slogan' means war cry.

Anger can be useful if you use anger and don't let it use you.

"Please avoid rhetoric. Say 'Duluth,' not 'the zenith city of the unsalted seas.' Say 'a small group of dishonest bosses,' not 'a miniscule coterie of unscrupulous elitists.' Don't revive words that were decently buried generations ago, or invent new ones. Don't say 'peers' when you mean 'equals,' or 'confidentiality' when you mean 'trust' or 'privacy.' And don't use nouns as adjectives or verbs."

Tash smiled. "So I can't say everybody who lives in a structured society has a conflicted personality?"

"Not unless you want to lose all thrust, clout, and charisma. Any other questions?"

"Only one. What are these speeches going to be about?"

Jeremy laughed aloud. He was beginning to seem more aware of her as an individual now.

"A difficult question!" The laughter lines faded. "The campaign starts tonight. I'm announcing my candidacy for a second term at a men's dinner for Nobel Prize winners at the University. From now on, there will be two major issues: inflation and the strike.

"There are only a few things you can do about inflation at the state level, but I'm going to do all of them. Carlos will brief you on details.

"As for the strike, I'm going to call one more conference with union leaders tomorrow. Don't laugh. It might work this time."

"And if it doesn't?"

His eyes went out of focus, looking into his own mind.

"I can't do what Carlos and Job want: shift the whole burden onto the President. The responsibility is mine, not his. I don't want to break a strike by injunction. It's a bad precedent. But how can I let this Barlovento blockade go on? If I do, people will starve in Barlovento next winter. That's war. That could mean a little Vietnam on our own front doorstep. I'll do anything to prevent that."

This morning, listening to Job Jackman's credo, Tash had begun to wonder if it was Jeremy Playfair's credo, too. If it was, she could not work for him. Now, listening to Jeremy himself, she realized that he had his own credo. It was not Job's. It was one Tash could respect. Job was evidently the tactician here, not the policy maker, perhaps not even the strategist.

"Anything else you want to know?"

"I can't think of anything, thank you."

Jeremy rose. "Back to the salt mines then. What's on this afternoon, Carlos?"

"A flock of bills that just passed the legislature before it adjourned."

"Important bills?" asked Hilary.

Carlos smiled. "Most people think the one abolishing capital punishment is fairly important."

"But you don't?" Job looked at Carlos quizzically.

Carlos shrugged. "I can't forget the hard-boiled Frenchman who said: *Que messieurs les assassins commencent!*"

"You know I don't speak French."

"Let murderers do it first."

"What else?" asked Hilary.

"There's that bill cracking down on drug addicts," said Carlos. "Jeremy is going to veto that."

Job turned on Jeremy. "You're making a double mistake: signing a bill to abolish the death penalty and vetoing a bill to crack down on drug addicts. Have you talked to Captain Wilkes about addicts? He's had a lot of experience."

"Wilkes is a post-dated Puritan."

51

"He's also an average voter. Better than a Gallup Poll any day. Jerry, the trick is to be liberal, but not too liberal. The middle of the road is where the votes are."

"We've got a new law that cracks down on drug pushers," said Jeremy. "One of the toughest in the country."

"The man in the street wants to crack down on pushers and addicts both," retorted Job. "He can't distinguish between them."

"But I can. Job, some day we'll have preventive law-enforcement, as we already have preventive medicine. Until we do we just have to compromise as best we can."

He gave good-bye to Jo Beth, nodded to Hilary and Tash, but paused when he came to his wife and took both her hands in his. "Take care of yourself, Viv. Promise!"

A glance from Hilary summoned Tash.

"It's three o'clock already. These luncheons kill the afternoon. I'd never get any work done if we had them often. What do you say to tennis and a swim?"

"That'll really kill the afternoon."

"You make your own hours here as long as you get things done on time. You can bone up on Barlovento this evening quite as well as this afternoon."

"I don't have a racket or sneakers, and this skirt is narrow."

"There are extra rackets for guests in the bathhouse. Sneakers and shorts, too."

Tash, long out of practise, was easily beaten by Hilary, but she enjoyed stretching her muscles. Even more, she enjoyed the swim afterward in a borrowed suit.

When she came out of the bathhouse, she found Hilary had ordered iced tea for both of them.

"Would you like a sandwich or something?" she asked Tash. "It's nearly six."

52

"I couldn't possibly eat anything after a late luncheon like that."

"Neither could I. Let's skip dinner and loaf here until the stars come out."

After so many months of living in town, Tash found herself luxuriating in the flower fragrances and the long reaches of new-mown grass gilded by a late afternoon sun.

"Is all this taxpayers' money?"

"A previous governor put in the tennis courts and the pool at his own expense. Jeremy pays for upkeep out of his own pocket. Like so many rich men in office, he is morbidly sensitive to any charge of freeloading, but then he can afford to be. It's the boy from the wrong side of the tracks who takes the taxpayer for every penny, but as he would be the first to point out, he has to, doesn't he?"

Walking back to the office wing through the soft spring night, Tash said: "Has Mrs. Playfair been ill?"

"What on earth makes you think that?"

"The way the Governor worries about her. Just now he said: 'Take care of yourself.' Monday he said: 'Are you sure you're not overdoing things?' "

"That's just his way. I'm an old friend of the Playfair family. My mother used to know his mother. I've never forgotten his mother saying years ago: 'Jerry was always such an affectionate little boy.' That quality is rare in men."

"You're a pessimist."

"Worse. A cynic. I believe in nothing, not even in the political future of Jeremy Playfair and that's high treason around here."

"Then why do you stay?"

"Because I love Jeremy. I can put it that way, because I'm old enough to be his mother. He has *mana.*"

"What's that?"

"The thing most people think they're talking about when they say charisma. It's Greek, selective and artificial, the gift of divine grace, sought by faith and bestowed by ritual on a priest or sacred king.

"*Mana* is Polynesian, unselective and natural, unsought and unbestowed. Every living creature is born with some *mana*. How could it be otherwise when *mana* is the power that makes and sustains the universe?"

"A Polynesian Holy Ghost?"

"I tried to find out, but the dictionary I consulted said simply: *The Holy Ghost. Obsolete.* So now I'll never know what the Holy Ghost is, or rather, was.

"Better stick to *mana*. It's the thing in all of us that works magic and is worked upon by magic, and it can't work without one's physical presence. A few people are born with more than their share of it. They cast spells on the rest of us. We go through life dancing to the tunes they play."

"And the Governor is one of those?"

Hilary nodded. "He has too much *mana*. He has too much of everything. Haven't you ever noticed how Fate loves a shining target? It's dangerous to be too lucky. Wasn't the Greek symbol for Nemesis a measure pressed down and running over?"

At the door of her own office Tash looked carefully at the array of alarm buttons. One glowed red. That meant the alarm system was working. She switched it off by pressing numbered buttons in the numerical sequence of the combination based on her birth date, and then opened the door.

"Hilary! Come here, please!"

"What's the matter?"

Tash had left her typewriter open. Now, something

54

yellow lay on the keys where she could not miss seeing it the moment she opened the door.

She had no words for what she felt as she stood looking down at the body of the dead canary.

Its neck was broken.

6

It was Hilary who found a piece of brown wrapping paper in the closet and made a parcel of the dead bird. It was Hilary who remembered to check the alarm button after she had locked the office door behind them with Tash's key.

"The alarm's working now. Was it working when you unlocked the door?"

"Yes. I switched it off before I used the key."

Hilary led the way down the corridor to the door that opened into the rest of the house.

"Could it have been a cat?" Tash could not quite control her voice.

"Would a cat leave a dead bird on a typewriter? And then go out of a room, shutting a door and resetting an alarm system? Whoever did all that walked on two legs."

"But why would anyone do it?"

They were crossing the broad front hall to a door Tash had not noticed before. Hilary opened it without knocking. A man in uniform was sitting at a switchboard with earphones on his head. He pushed the earphones aside as Hilary began to speak.

"Tell Captain Wilkes that Mrs. Truance must see him at once. Priority. I'll wait here in the hall until he comes."

"Shouldn't we tell Mrs. Playfair?" said Tash.

"She's resting," said Hilary. "She skipped dinner, too. I think we should let her rest."

The hall was empty and shadowy as they sat down to wait for Captain Wilkes.

"I didn't realize there were so many policemen here," said Tash.

"It's the Governor's guard, detailed from the state police. There are a dozen of them, but sometimes I think that's not enough. Obviously, it wasn't enough today."

"Why are you so sure this was someone from outside? Couldn't it have been an inside job, a wanton joke? One of the pages perhaps? Or somebody in the kitchen?"

Hilary shook her head. "I doubt it. They're all hand-picked. They're all civil servants. They're well-paid and they've always seemed proud of their jobs."

"What is Captain Wilkes like?"

"He's hand-picked, too. Command of the Governor's guard, is the plum job for state policemen, and Captain Wilkes is not a stereotype. He's a West Point graduate who took degrees in law and criminology after he left the Army. Bred to be a soldier, he believes that war is a collective psychosis, epidemic in the twentieth century, and that civilian crime is merely one phase of the disease."

"Do you think he's right?"

"I don't know, but if he's wrong, I hope no one ever tells him so. Captain Wilkes would take it hard, and—"

She was cut short by the front doorbell.

An usher crossed the hall and opened the door to two men in uniform.

The cavalry breeches and boots reminded Tash that when the state police service was founded there were no cars. The men had patrolled on horseback, like Canadian Mounted Police from whom their uniforms were copied.

There had been a lot of resistance to taking them off

57

horses, but it finally became apparent to everyone that they could not gallop after modern cars in a state that comprised ten thousand square miles. Their first cars were big sedans, and their first radios took up the whole back seat. Now they had small, fast cars and two-way radios they could carry in their pockets, but they still wore cavalry boots and breeches and officers still called their men troopers.

"Captain Wilkes!" Hilary almost ran to the older of the two men. "Look." She opened the brown paper parcel. "It was in Miss Perkins office, on her typewriter. We found it a few moments ago. Before we went into the office, the door was locked and the alarm system was working."

"Miss Perkins?" He bowed to Tash. "You're assuming this is Mrs. Playfair's canary?"

"I know it is."

"Let's make sure." He turned to the younger man beside him. "Lieutenant Pulaski, you know where the Florida Room is. If the cage is empty, bring it here." He turned back to Hilary.

"Does Mrs. Playfair know?"

"No."

"Then let's wrap this up again." He folded the paper around the dead bird. "I wouldn't want her to come downstairs and see it suddenly, without any warning."

Pulaski came back carrying the cage. There was still sand on the floor and pieces of lettuce and cuttlebone. There were still bowls of seed and water, but the door stood open and the cage was empty. No bright-eyed, little ball of feathers mopped and mowed before the scrap of looking-glass or poured out his heart in song.

"Be careful how you handle that cage," said Wilkes. "I know it's mostly wicker, but there's some smooth wood in the frame. There just might be a fingerprint. Send it down to the lab with this parcel, mark both *Immediate Attention*, and send four men to search every room in this house. It's barely possible that whoever did it is still here, though it's not likely.

"One other thing: Call the company that installed the alarm system and tell them we want a technician to come here and check it at once."

"It couldn't be bypassed, could it?" said Hilary.

"That's what I want to find out. It's an old system, installed years ago. I've been telling the Governor that he should demand a more modern one. This doesn't have any of the latest gimmicks. For instance, it doesn't have a back-up system working on long-term batteries to switch to automatically if the electricity goes off in a storm."

"Anything else, sir?"

"Yes, I want you yourself to check the men on the gates. Ask each one for names and descriptions of every-body who came in or went out since—" He turned back to Hilary. "When did anyone last see the bird alive?"

"Before luncheon, I think. A little after one. Tash and I have been with each other ever since one."

"And just when did you find the bird?"

"About ten minutes ago."

Wilkes turned back to Pulaski.

"That narrows it a little. We must identify everyone who went in or out of this place between one and five this afternoon. I also want to know if there were any untoward incidents at the gates, like someone trying to get in or out without proper identification."

The lieutenant was starting to salute when Wilkes' voice arrested his motion.

"Pulaski."

"Sir?"

Wilkes looked at his watch. "It's nine o'clock. The

Governor is already at that Nobel Prize dinner, making a speech to announce his candidacy. Tell the man on the switchboard here to call the University and ask for one of the Governor's aides—preferably Mr. de Miranda. Try not to alarm him unnecessarily, but tell him that if it's at all possible for him to get back here at once without inconveniencing the Governor, I'd appreciate it."

"Yes, sir." This time Pulaski finished his salute and pivoted on his heel.

"Mrs. Truance, do you think this can be kept out of the newspapers?" demanded Wilkes.

"If anybody can do it, Carlos de Miranda will."

"He must do it. We'll never find this hole in our security if we've got a gaggle of reporters on our heels."

It gave a Tash a funny feeling to realize that she was no longer an outsider, one of the gaggle of reporters. She was now an insider, hoping that those dreadful newspaper people would not get hold of this incident and blow it up out of all proportion to its significance.

At the same time, she couldn't help wishing that she could talk over the whole thing with Bill Brewer. How interested he would be and how his comments would throw light into the dark corners!

"Could the bird have got out of the cage by itself?" Tash was thinking aloud now. "Or could someone have let it out and then become too frightened to report it when the bird got away? Don't birds indoors dash themselves to death against windowpanes trying to get through the glass they can't see?"

"You're suggesting that the bird killed himself and then someone who found the body put it on your typewriter?"

Tash nodded.

"Miss Perkins, did you look closely at that bird?"

"No, I couldn't bear to."

"It didn't die by beating its head against a window-pane. Its neck was twisted. It was strangled the way a farmer's wife strangles a chicken—with hands. I doubt if we can get any fingerprints off the feathers, but we may get a trace of bodily secretion—sweat or saliva—or a pulled thread from a frayed cuff. Such things can be used for identification. That's why I sent the bird to the lab with everything else."

"But what could the motive be?" demanded Hilary. "Just to frighten Mrs. Playfair or Miss Perkins?"

Wilkes' face stiffened like something that had been melted, now hardening as it chilled.

"You don't need motives if drug addicts are involved. They tear down their own minds deliberately, psycho-analysis in reverse. Sometimes I almost wish we had a whipping post the way they used to over the Border in Delaware."

"You can't regard flogging as a civilized deterrent," Hilary spoke with the detachment of an anthropologist inspecting a peculiar tribal custom.

"We could call it aversion therapy, if that would make it sound more civilized," retorted Wilkes. "It's only a bird this time, but next time it could just as easily be a child. An atrocity against an animal is just a warm-up for an atrocity against a human being. There's a case in Hans Gross records of a man who couldn't achieve plea-sure unless he strangled a bird during coition. Of course the time came when he strangled the woman instead of the bird. It always does."

"Then you think a pervert broke in and strangled the bird just for kicks without malice toward any of us?"

"Either that or strangling the bird was a perverted reaction to the tension of breaking in the way you or I would light a cigarette."

"But it was so stupid!" cried Tash. "If he hadn't strangled the bird we would never have known anyone had broken in."

"Which is another reason for thinking the whole thing was psychopathic," said Wilkes. "The only motive I can see for this is a psycho's desire to shock or disgust somebody."

"I can think of another motive," said Hilary. "We're on the eve of an election. There are all kinds of position papers and projected schedules about future policies lying around the office wing. They might be salable to newspapers or stock market speculators or even opposition candidates. In that case, the bird would be strangled just to make us think a psycho did it."

"I am more interested in how he got in than why he got in," said Wilkes. "Miss Perkins, was your burglar alarm on when you left your office to go to luncheon?"

"Yes, it was."

"Was it still on when you came back to the office?"

"Yes."

"Then I can't understand how anyone got in and out of your office without the alarm going off. Did anyone else know the combination?"

"Only Mr. de Miranda who showed me how to set it this morning."

"One last question," said Wilkes. "Has anything out of the ordinary happened here the last few days?"

"Everything that happens here is out of the ordinary."

"That's not what I mean and I think you know it, Mrs. Truance."

"Something out of the ordinary happened to me before I came here." Tash hadn't meant to volunteer information, but the words popped out of her mouth as if they had an independent life of their own. "My pocket was picked."

"Oh?" Captain Wilkes collected himself like a pointer dog on point. "Did you report this?"

"Yes, at the precinct station house near my home. They showed me mug shots, and I identified one of the pickpockets, a man with a cast in one eye. It made his face look lopsided, like a gibbous moon. The other was just a boy. They didn't have photos of him."

"What did you lose?"

"Thirty-nine dollars and a wallet containing a blank check and an identity card."

She knew she ought to add: *and a letter Mrs. Playfair asked me to mail,* but she didn't. The role of tattletale was too distasteful.

"Did they tell you the names of these characters?"

"The man was a Barloventan known as Halcón and the boy was one of his chicks or *polluelitos* known as Freaky."

"Oh!" Hilary was distressed.

"I see you know what a chicken hawk is," said Wilkes.

"But I don't," said Tash.

"A chicken hawk is a man who traffics in young boy prostitutes, the younger the better. He has his heterosexual counterpart, of course, and both are under the protection of the Family, our cozy, domestic name for organized crime in this state.

Silently, Lieutenant Pulaski materialized at his captain's elbow, but it was Tash he addressed.

"Is this yours, ma'am?" A coin lay in the palm of his hand, a bright new copper penny. "I found it on the floor in your office."

"I don't think it's mine," said Tash. "But I suppose I could have dropped it there this morning without noticing."

"There's nothing much more to report, sir," Pulaski told Wilkes. "Mr. de Miranda says both he and the Governor will be here as soon as the Governor finishes making his speech, probably around ten o'clock."

"It's nearly ten now. Anything else?"

"No unauthorized person tried to get past any of the sentries today. There is no evidence that any circuits in the alarm system have been tampered with, and no signs of housebreaking at any door or window."

"What about the men searching the house?"

"They've found nothing so far, sir. No sign of any intruder."

Tash and Hilary looked at one another. It was Hilary who found voice: "If you're suggesting that someone here in the household strangled a pet of Mrs. Playfair's, I just don't believe that's possible."

"Perhaps not," said Wilkes. "But isn't it possible that someone in the household might have let in someone else who did the strangling? A mechanical security system is only as strong as its weakest human link."

They all heard the crunch of the gravel under wheels in the driveway.

The usher who opened the door stood aside to let Jeremy and Carlos enter. They looked festive, debonair, and old-fashioned in the contrasting blacks and whites of full evening dress.

Whatever Carlos had said, Jeremy assumed something was wrong with Vivian. His eyes went to Hilary. "Is she ill?"

"No, nothing like that," said Hilary. "But we have something to tell you before you see her."

"What is it?"

"Her canary is dead."

"Her canary!" Jeremy laughed with relief. "Poor, old Blondel! I thought he had at least another five years to go, but—"

"Jerry, you don't understand. Blondel didn't just die. He was killed. Strangled and left on Tash Perkins' typewriter."

"Governor," said Wilkes. "Somebody got in from outside. At least, we think that must be it, but the alarm system didn't go off, and none of the sentries saw any-body."

"Does Mrs. Playfair know?"

"Not yet."

Jeremy turned to Carlos. "Will you take over here for a few minutes? Vivian must be told, and I want to break it to her myself."

He ran lightly up the wide curving staircase.

Carlos became all Spanish now. The distress of his friend Jeremy made him furious, but the fury was frigidly controlled.

"Captain Wilkes."

"Sir."

"How do you account for this?"

"I cannot account for it yet, sir."

"Will you kindly have the goodness to start at the beginning and tell me everything that has happened so I can report it to the Governor in detail as soon as possible?"

"Carlos, don't you think we might all sit down?" said Hilary plaintively.

Carlos moved a chair out from the wall for Hilary, and Tash quickly perched on another, but Carlos himself remained standing and Wilkes felt obliged to follow suit.

He was nearly at the end of his story when there were footsteps on the stair.

Tash looked up.

The Governor was coming down alone. His quick movements, slight figure, and tousled hair contributed to an illusion of boyishness until you saw his eyes.

He stopped on the bottom step. His glance fled from Wilkes to Hilary to Tash and came to rest on Carlos.

His voice was husky.

"She isn't there. I can't find her anywhere. No one has seen her since luncheon."

7

IN THE NEXT half hour Captain Wilkes and his men established that Vivian was not in the house or on the grounds, and that her small, open car was not in the garage.

She had not vanished through a black hole into a counter-universe of antimatter. She had gone away in a car driven by an engine fueled with gas.

The only uncanny thing was the stubborn fact that none of the sentries guarding roads in and out of Leafy Way had seen her leave.

Leafy Way had been laid out long before any need for tight security. There was no wall, no electrified fences, just hedges. Anyone could get in or out of the grounds on foot, but how could anyone get out by car when there was a sentry box by each carriage gate?

Wilkes wanted to know if he should assume she had left of her own free will.

Jeremy looked at Carlos helplessly. "What do you think?"

Carlos' shoulders moved skeptically. "Who knows?"

"Has anything like this ever happened before, Governor?" said Wilkes.

"Nothing quite like this."

"There have been rumors." Wilkes paused tactfully.

"What rumors? Don't pull punches."

"Rumors that Mrs. Playfair is in the habit of absenting herself from her family without explanation."

"You may deny those rumors."

"No doubt I shall soon have the opportunity. You do realize, sir, that we cannot keep this disappearance from the press? We will have to send out a five-state alarm. I could not take the responsibility for not doing so, but such an alarm is news when it involves a governor's wife. Big news."

"Yes, of course, I see that, but you don't have to tell the press every detail. This business about the canary. The possibility that she may have left impulsively without telling anyone. There's no point in mentioning either one of those things to the press."

Tash had a sense of the dreadful unspoken, the shadows in every life that must never be put into words or even thought, the ghosts at the back of every mind.

Was Jeremy trying to defend the indefensible? Was he ruthlessly smothering his own unbearable suspicion that Vivian was responsible for everything, even the strangling of her own canary?

"We'll have to tell them the car is missing," said Wilkes. "State and city police must have a full description of that car. And we must get the alarm out now. For Mrs. Playfair's own sake, we can't afford to wait another second."

"You're right," said Jeremy. "Do it at once. Carlos, call a press conference to be held here in an hour."

"Let me take the first barrage," said Carlos. "I'll meet them with a written statement. You can put in a brief appearance at the last minute confirming what I've said."

"Don't you think I could stand up to the first barrage?"

"I'm sure you could, but why bother when you don't

67

have to? This is going to be rough. The slightest slip of the tongue, even the slightest hesitation, and they'll be on you like a pack of hounds on a wounded hare. Save your strength for tomorrow when you may really need it."

Hilary nodded to Carlos. "I'll see he gets some rest."

"Rest?" Jeremy's scorn flashed out like a whiplash. "Do you think I can rest now? If anybody needs me I'll be with Wilkes in the communications room. That's where news will come first."

Carlos sighed. "Tash, you and I have work to do and only an hour to do it in. We use the Florida Room for press conferences here, because it's big and secluded from the rest of the house. We'll need a telephone there."

He unplugged an extension from the wall.

"Let's go."

The Florida Room was in darkness. Carlos switched on chandeliers and sconces, plugged in the telephone he was carrying, and dialed the Leafy Way switchboard operator.

"Nick? Miranda here. If there are any calls for me or Miss Perkins in the next hour, we'll be in the Florida Room. Call the press room at the State House and tell every correspondent there that the Governor is having a press conference here at eleven o'clock. Better call the wire services, too. Tell the chief usher that everyone is to be shown directly to the Florida Room. We don't want them straying all over the house. Call whoever is on night duty at the secretariat and tell her to stand by for a typing and Xerox job in a few minutes. Tell one of the pages to bring a tape recorder to the Florida Room now."

Tash looked at her watch. "Ten after ten already."

"Time enough if we don't hurry," returned Carlos. "You Saxons in North America are always hurrying."

"You mean Anglo-Saxons?"

"Same thing. Now please stop hurrying so I can think a little."

"Saxons can't stop hurrying," said Tash. "It's in our genes. The ice age and all that. If we hadn't hurried then, we would have been extinct."

She stopped as she realized Carlos was not listening. "Miss Perkins—"

"You said 'Tash' a moment ago."

"Did I? All right, Tash. What do you think has happened to Mrs. Playfair?"

"How can I possibly say? I've been a member of this household less than twenty-four hours."

"So you have a fresh point of view, and that's why I'm asking you. Jerry and I are so close to her, we can't see her as she really is. What do you think of her?"

"She's beautiful but somehow tragic. I don't know why."

"Tragic?" He tasted the word. "You think she's not happy?"

"She ought to be."

"That's no answer. Did she seem happy to you the first day you met her?"

"No, but she did today. At luncheon she was radiant."

Carlos started to offer her a cigarette. "Oh, I forgot. You don't smoke." He lit one for himself. "In a small, closed official household like this you never know what is being said in the real world outside. Tell me: Do people in town gossip about Vivian?"

"There have been rumors that she disappears every now and then for no known reason. My editor briefed me on this before I came here to interview her."

Carlos lit another cigarette, forgetting the one already burning in the ashtray. He lifted his chin to blow out a long plume of smoke toward the ceiling, then brought his eyes down to Tash again.

"It has happened. Three times. We don't know where she goes or what she does. Her explanations are what lawyers call 'frivolous and irrelevant.' The only people who are supposed to know about this at all are those closest to her."

"And they are?"

"Her husband. Me, because I'm close to him. Her social secretary, Hilary. And her maid, Juana, whom you haven't met. When Vivian disappears we four close ranks and cover up for her, but we didn't do a very good job of it tonight. The canary business unnerved Hilary. Nothing like that has ever happened before."

"But she always comes back unharmed?"

"She has in the past."

"And you can't even guess where she goes or what she does?"

Carlos' answer was dragged out of him. "Perhaps I don't want to guess."

"Oh, Carlos, don't you think the police should be told everything now? That strangling of her pet bird may be a symbolic threat of violence against her. She may be in danger."

"She doesn't behave like a frightened woman. Each time she has gone away she has always come back in good health and spirits. Each time, she's insisted that it would never happen again."

"But it has. Couldn't you tell the police all this without telling the press?"

"You've just told me your editor knows about her disappearances already. We thought that was a secret we had kept. Did he say anything else about Vivian?"

"No, he didn't, but something happened to me which I think the police ought to know about now. There was a letter—"

The door opened. A page came in with a tape recording machine.

70

"On the coffee table," said Carlos.

"Anything else, sir?"

"That's all, thank you."

The door closed. Carlos turned back to Tash.

"What's this about a letter?"

"The day I interviewed Mrs. Playfair she gave me a letter to mail for her. Then, when you and the Governor appeared and I mentioned the letter to her, she said, 'I don't know what you are talking about.' This morning I tried to speak about the letter again. Twice. The first time she changed the subject. The second time she said she didn't want to talk about it."

"When did you mail the letter?"

"I never got a chance to mail it. My pocket was picked after I left here. The pickpockets took her letter when they took my wallet."

"Does she know the letter was stolen?"

"No. That's what I was trying to tell her when she refused to talk about the letter. I couldn't have forced her to listen without making a scene. There were other people there. It was just before luncheon."

"Did you notice the name and address on the letter?"

"Not really. I just noticed that it was addressed to a Doctor, not to a Mr. or Mrs. or Ms. Don't you think we'd better get that press release blocked out now?"

Carlos looked at his watch. "Dios! Only forty minutes left! We'll both have to be Saxon now and hurry. I'll dictate. You stop me and smooth out any rough places as we go along. Remember, this must be all clichés. They're so reassuring. Ready?"

"Ready."

Carlos narrowed his eyes against the cloud of cigarette smoke around his head.

"State and city police are sending out a five-state alarm here tonight for Mrs. Jeremy Playfair, wife of the Governor, who has been missing from the residence at Leafy Way since . . . Since when?"

"It was about ten when the Governor discovered she was missing, but no one has seen her since three when the luncheon party broke up."

"We'd better say 'since shortly after two o'clock.' The longer she's been missing, the more likely people are to pay attention to this. What happened to the mike? Thanks." Carlos backed up the tape, erased the last words, and re-dictated. ". . . since shortly after two o'clock this afternoon. Her car, a white covertible . . . Do you remember the make and year?"

"Buick, 1975."

"A Buick, 1975, is also missing. She was last seen at a luncheon party today at Leafy Way attended by . . . Who was there?"

Tash spoke directly into the microphone. "The Governor himself, members of his staff, and the Lieutenant Governor and Mrs. Jackman."

Carlos took back the microphone. "All those who saw her at luncheon agree that she appeared to be in normal health and spirits at that time, but—"

"Stop! I'd say 'usual' instead of 'normal,' because normal always suggests its opposite, abnormal, is lurking in the wings."

"Good point. In her usual health and spirits at that time. Hospital emergency wards are being checked throughout city and state, but so far there is no indication that Mrs. Playfair has met with an accident. There remains the possibility that she may be the victim of an unreported accident, or that she is suffering from loss of memory. Anyone with any knowledge of her whereabouts should telephone the Governor's house at Leafy Way or State Police Headquarters immediately at one of the following numbers. We'll get the numbers from the switchboard. Any criticism?"

"You want the truth?"

"Yes."

"The whole thing sounds fake. People will never understand why we are sending out a five-state alarm at ten when she's only been missing since two. We need something to make it more real. Since we can't tell the whole truth, her previous disappearances and the canary business, we need something else to make it sound like an emergency. What about her engagements this afternoon? Did she break any?"

"Hilary will know." Carlos reached for the telephone. He was smiling when he put it down. "She had a private engagement. An old school friend coming to tea at five."

"And she broke it?"

"No, much better. She failed to keep it without breaking it. That's the sort of detail that makes a disappearance seem involuntary, which is the very effect we want to create."

Carlos dialed the switchboard again. "Nick, I need all the telephone numbers for Leafy Way and the state police barracks, and a page to take a tape to the secretariat for Xeroxing."

When the page came back with Xeroxes of the transcript made from the tape recording, Carlos said, "If you'll proofread these, I'll go and tell Jerry about that letter of Vivian's that was stolen. I think he ought to know."

"Will you be back in time to meet the newspapermen?"

"I'll be back in two minutes."

The door crashed behind him as he plunged out of the room.

So he can hurry if he wants to. Tash filled in the telephone numbers on the Xeroxes by hand in order to save time. She had just finished when Carlos burst back into the room.

73

"Too late! They're here. I didn't even get as far as Jerry. Some day, when this is all over, I shall go back to my mother's house in Sotavento and spend the rest of my life in the sun translating the love poetry of pre-Islamic Arabs into Spanish. I am not Saxon. I do not like hurrying."

The chief usher appeared in the door way to announce the newspaper men.

Carlos dropped his cigarette stub in an ashtray, threw back his shoulders, and took up his stance in front of the fireplace. Now he was another person. Gone was the anxious, harassed public relations man, fussing over a tricky press release that had to repress more than it released. Now he was the embodiment of *sangré azul*, which always sounds so much more romantic than blue blood.

The tawny marble of the chimney piece threw his dark good looks into high relief. The sense of failure he had expressed a only a moment ago might never have existed. He seemed serenely assured that he could command the respect of a press corps that made a cult of irreverence. And if anybody can, he will, thought Tash.

The reporters fanned out until they formed a semicircle around him.

"Good evening," he said. "Most of you know Miss Perkins. She has a written statement for you."

Tash went through the crowd, handing out Xeroxed sheets. When she reached the other side of the room, she was amazed to see Bill Brewer.

"Once a reporter always a reporter?"

"I get tired of sitting at a desk all day every day," he answered. "Besides, I wanted to see you. Like it here?"

"Never a dull moment."

"But you don't smile when you say that."

"I don't feel like smiling tonight. This disappearance is frightening."

74

"Any idea what's behind it?"

"None whatever."

"How about dinner with me when this is over?"

"Thanks, but I'm needed here tonight."

"Tomorrow?"

"I'd like that. Bill, who are all these men? I don't recognize half of them."

"Some of the Washington press corps came down for this."

"Why?"

"You ask why, and you a newspaper woman? Playfair is news. Just in the last few days there have been four big stories about him on the front page of every paper. He's abolished the death penalty. He's trying to end a strike that could to lead to riots in the *barrio* or war in the Caribbean. He's announced his candidacy for a second term as governor, and now his wife has disappeared. If he survives all this, he'll be President in a few years, and we all know it. That fellow trying to catch Miranda's eye now is the top Washington man for *The New York Times.*"

"Yes?" said Carlos.

"Is there any truth in the rumor that Mrs. Playfair has disappeared before and returned without explanation?"

"No truth whatsoever."

The simple honesty in Carlos' voice and expression would have convinced Tash that he was telling the truth if she had not happened to know that he was lying.

Apparently, he did convince the *Times* man, but a woman reporter was more suspicious.

"Is Mrs. Playfair subject to attacks of amnesia?"

"No."

"Could she be visiting a friend unofficially?"

"That's a nasty one," whispered Bill. "Might as well ask right out if she has a lover."

"No." Carlos still managed to keep his voice detached and remote.

"Is she subject to dizzy spells or allergies?"

Bill translated sotto voce: "Does she get drunk?"

"No."

Now it was the turn of a little man in the back of the room. *"Christian Science Monitor,"* muttered Bill.

To those in front where Tash was standing, the little man was invisible, just a disembodied voice floating over the heads of taller men.

"What happened to the canary?"

Carlos almost cracked, then made a supreme effort: "I beg your pardon, I don't understand you."

"The last time I was in this room there was a canary in a big wicker cage. It belonged to Mrs. Playfair and it was called Blondel. Where is it now?"

"Mrs. Playfair has had the bird moved to her sitting room upstairs. And now, if there are no further questions, the Governor has a word to say to you."

"I'll see if he's ready," said Tash.

The hall was empty. She found Jeremy and Hilary in the communications room. He rose.

"Time for me?"

"Yes. Any news?"

"Nothing."

He had himself under control, but there were lines in his face that Tash had never seen there before.

The bright lights of the Florida Room did not spare him as he stood beside Carlos and smiled at one or two of the reporters whom he knew well.

"I decided to hold this press conference instead of merely announcing Mrs. Playfair's disappearance, because I wanted to ask you personally for your help. You have many sources of information, and perhaps some that are not available to me or the police. I shall welcome with gratitude anything you can do or suggest to help me find my wife."

He fielded one or two questions with the ease of long

76

practice. There was nothing even resembling cross-examination. The sympathy of the crowd had been with him from the moment he entered the room.

He does have *mana*, thought Tash. His mere physical presence is winning them over now as all Carlos' urbanity and address could not do.

As the last reporter filed out, Hilary came in.

"The police want to talk to all of us again," she said. "What are we going to tell them?"

"The truth," said Carlos. "The whole truth."

Jeremy looked up sharply. "Without holding anything back?"

"Holding things back now will just make it harder if we have to tell everything in the end, as we undoubtedly shall."

"But what about Vivian? Do you think telling the police everything is best for her?"

"Don't you?"

"While you're making up your minds, I'm going to ring for sandwiches and drinks and coffee," said Hilary.

The others protested that they were neither hungry nor thirsty, yet, when the picnic supper arrived, they all began to sip and nibble.

Suddenly, Jeremy broke away from Carlos.

"All right. You've convinced me. The police shall be told everything now, warts and all. Find Wilkes and ask him to step over here."

Carlos left the room, shutting the door quietly this time.

"Would you like Tash and me to leave?" asked Hilary.

"No." Jeremy smiled. "I have no secrets from Tash or you."

There was a tap on one of the French windows. Tash parted the curtains and saw Carlos on the other side of the glass. She opened the window.

"Jerry!" Carlos' voice was low and urgent. "There's a

77

car coming up the old right of way through the orchard. You don't want a guard to stop her, do you?"

"Her?"

"It's a white convertible, and—"

Already Jeremy was outside the window, Carlos at his heels. Tash and Hilary followed, hurrying around the East Wing to the orchard.

"The old right of way!" cried Hilary. "It's an unpaved lane, so neglected and overgrown for years I didn't even think a car could get through, but I should have remembered it."

"So should I," said Tash. "Sam Bates told me about it the first time I came here."

"There's always a disused place that everybody forgets," said Hilary. "That's how the Dauphin was smuggled out of the Temple, to vanish forever during the French Revolution."

The forgotten lane was deep in shadow under the trees. The car coming toward them so slowly was visible in the moonlight only because it was white.

There was a curve in the lane. The car did not follow the curve. It left the lane and kept on coming toward the house over the grass slowly as if it were rolling in neutral down a slight incline under its own momentum. As it came nearer they could see that the one occupant was in the driver's seat, but the hands slid off steering wheel while the car was still moving.

Jeremy ran across the grass. The others followed. Evening dew soaked their ankles.

Jeremy got to the car first. It was still moving slowly. He ran beside it, reaching for the hand brake. The car lurched to a stop.

It was she, slumped in one corner of the driver's seat, eyes closed, head on her own shoulder, fair hair drifting across her face. There was a bruise on her forehead, bleeding a little.

Jeremy opened the car door. Without a word, he lifted her out of the car, cradled her in his arms, and carried her over the grass to the house.

"Look," said Carlos.

On one side, the whole length of the car was scored with a deep gash from front headlight to rear fender. It looked like a sheet of paper that had been slashed savagely with a bowie knife.

"What could have done that?" cried Tash.

"Some projection that struck the car when it was moving at high speed, sharp enough to plow through its skin of thin modern steel," said Carlos.

"I've seen other scars like that before," said Hilary. "They happen most often if you try to pass a truck at high speed when you're shaving it too close. Another millimeter and that would have killed her. I wonder if she was conscious when it happened."

"Probably not fully conscious, but the other driver may have been. Let's hope it was too dark for him to read her license plate."

8

TASH WOKE AT dawn next morning. While she dressed, she listened to news on the radio.

"Vivian Playfair, the Governor's wife, who was reported missing yesterday, returned to Leafy Way late last night. Carlos de Miranda, the Governor's A.D.C., told newsmen that it was all a misunderstanding, and Mrs. Playfair is deeply distressed by the anxiety she may have caused for a few hours. The Orioles . . ."

It was still early when Tash left her car in the executive office parking lot. The day was windless, the landscape still as a painting. Birds called to each other in the trees above her head, and sun filtered through the leaves. It would be hot in an hour, but now the delicious freshness of dawn lingered in the mild air.

It came to her then that beauty and peace are largely aspects of vegetable life and inanimate nature. The moment the animal appears, even in his humblest forms, ugliness and war take over. What was an animal but appetite? A mouth, a maw, and a clutch of eggs and sperm feeding on one another?

Such thoughts do not come to people who are happy, especially on a beautiful spring morning. Why was she unhappy?

She met Hilary in the corridor of the office wing.

"I was looking for you. Vivian wants to see you. She's upstairs."

They passed through the door to the rest of the house and went up the wide stairway. Hilary led the way down the central corridor and knocked on a door.

"Come in!"

The door was opened by a young woman in a black dress with a black silk apron. One look at her face told Tash that this was Juana. "Monstrously scarred," Jo Beth had said. It was worse than that. The whole face was puckered on one side by a cruel scar that ran from hairline to chin.

No wonder she had emigrated to America. To live with a face like that in Barlovento, where sex was still a woman's only value must have left far more monstrous scars on the mind, however invisible. Tash was almost afraid to think of the banked fires that must burn secretly night and day under her unnaturally self-effacing manner.

Opaque curtains were drawn across every window in the bedroom. Only one lamp was burning. Its shaded light fused all the pale colors of the room into a gray monotone.

Vivian was sitting up in a wide bed, propped against a pile of pillows, smoking a cigarette. Even her fair hair and lacy bed jacket looked gray in that treacherous light. Once more her eyes were dull and her face lax and old-looking as they had been the first time Tash saw her. There was a patch of surgical tape on one temple.

She made an effort to smile, but it wavered and collapsed. "I've caused so much trouble," she said. "I'm sorry."

"I'm glad to see you back. There's really nothing to be sorry for."

81

"Oh, but there is. I should have left word that I was going out. I just didn't remember to do so. That's my trouble. I don't remember things. You are not going to believe this. Nobody else does, but it's the truth. I simply do not remember anything that happened yesterday afternoon or evening. I remember going upstairs to rest after luncheon, and the next thing I remember is Jerry carrying me over the lawn to the house last night. Everything in between is blank. This morning they told me about the damage to the car, but I have no idea how it happened."

There are two classic responses for the reluctant witness: *I don't know* and *I don't remember.* Vivian had chosen the second. No one was likely to suffer such a sudden and extensive loss of memory as she claimed without a blow on the head or a great emotional shock or a great deal of alcohol.

There had been no bruise on her temple at luncheon. That wound had surely been acquired at the same time as the gash on the body of the car. Both must have occurred after she left the house, yet she had just claimed she could not remember leaving the house. She had had only one martini before luncheon. So far as Tash could recall, nothing had happened at luncheon likely to induce emotional shock in her.

This was what Washington called a cover-up. It left Tash wondering more than ever what could lie underneath.

"I asked to see you because I wanted to explain about that letter," said Vivian. "You don't have to worry about its being stolen. It wasn't important. Just a letter to one of those mail order houses that advertise gadgets. This was a miniature watering pot, a silly hand-painted thing that would add a little gaiety to dull jobs like watering indoor plants. I should have told you that before."

82

This time she achieved a ghost of her old smile.

Tash tried to summon an answering smile. "Don't worry, please. It doesn't matter."

Vivian looked about for an ashtray and found one under a fold of the frilly counterpane. She stubbed out her cigarette and lit another.

"Wouldn't it be safer to keep the ashtray on the bedside table?" suggested Tash.

"I suppose so, but that's so far to reach in a bed as wide as this. I haven't the energy . . ."

Downstairs in Tash's office, Hilary lit a cigarette of her own. "Well?"

"You expect me to believe that?"

"Nobody believes it."

"What did happen?"

"I have no way of knowing."

"What do you think?"

"I can't think at this point. I can only guess. Could it be an alcoholic blackout?"

"It's hard to believe that anyone as much in the public eye as Vivian Playfair could be a secret drinker without being detected long ago."

"There's more than one kind of alcoholism," returned Hilary. "It can be periodic. That's the kind that's easiest to conceal for any length of time. Some of them can go for weeks or months without alcohol and then, suddenly, they have to spend a few days drinking themselves blind. And it can happen to those who have everything to live for, at least, apparently."

"You're sure?"

"I'm sure. It happened to my husband."

It was the first glimpse that Tash had had into the long past that must have shaped Hilary's present. How differently we would feel about people if they could carry visible pasts around with them . . .

"Every few months he used to drink himself into a blackout," said Hilary. "And he always insisted on driving when he was blacked out. That's what killed him. When I saw the gash on Vivian's car last night, and the bruise on her forehead, I remembered one night when he came home with a crushed fender and a broken head. He hadn't the slightest idea of what he had hit or how he had pulled out of it or where he had been."

"That would explain her periodic absences," said Tash. "Going off some place to drink by herself. She couldn't do that here. And it might explain those periodic changes in her appearance. Not illnesss, just a colossal hangover. But what about that letter she gave me to mail?"

"Writing to someone who supplies her with liquor and a place to drink it in privacy, trying to hide the fact from Jeremy."

"You think he knows now?"

"He must suspect something by this time."

"How could she be such a fool?"

Hilary lit another cigarette. "Who knows? The surface of life gives little indication of what lies underneath until something like this happens. I used to think I had made my husband happy. Obviously, I hadn't. I've always thought Jeremy had made Vivian happy, but perhaps he hasn't."

"There are cures, aren't there?"

"Oh, yes. Sometimes they work, and sometimes they don't. My husband tried everything: psychoanalysis, hypnosis, group therapy, biochemical therapy, antabuse. Everything. Nothing worked."

"If she continues this way, she'll destroy him."

Hilary nodded.

"If it comes out—as it almost certainly will in an election campaign—people may feel sorry for Jeremy, but they won't vote for him. Not even if he divorced her."

"He won't divorce her," said Tash.

"Why not?"

"He is not the kind of man who would desert a wife in trouble when she needs him most."

"I wonder if voters would feel the way you do?"

"Women voters would."

"Then God help Jerry! If this comes out, he's locked into disaster."

"What do you mean?"

"If he goes on living with her, the taint will rub off on him. Some men will think he's weak, others will wonder if he drove her to it. But if he divorces her, women like you will say he deserted a wife in trouble in order to save his career. Politically, he's damned if he leaves her, and damned if he doesn't."

"We're just guessing," said Tash. "This may not be the truth at all.

"Want to bet? She's going into a private nursing home day after tomorrow. For a checkup. At least that's what the press release will say. Tash, I wouldn't blame you if you resigned now. There's not going to be any future in politics for anyone who worked for Jeremy Playfair."

"I'm not in politics."

Hilary's eyes grew pensive. "So, like the rest of us, you've fallen for the Playfair *mana.*"

"Bunk!" Tash spoke as crisply as she could. "To me this is just an interesting job. Material for my future memoirs."

Hilary didn't bother to answer such nonsense. There was a pen in her hand and she was drawing high-heeled shoes all over Tash's engagement pad.

"If you're going to stay, you'd better move in here pretty soon. Now Jerry has announced his candidacy, we'll be in the campaign before we know it, and you won't have time to commute between Leafy Way and your apartment. You'll be working twenty-four hours a day."

"All right." Tash rose. "I'm dining out this evening, but after dinner I'll go home and pack a bag and come back here. It'll be a nice change from a newspaper office, where you work thirty-four hours a day."

Hilary was halfway to the door when Tash stopped her.

"There's one thing we've forgotten."

"What?"

"The canary. Alcoholism wouldn't explain that."

"No," said Hilary. "Nothing we know explains that."

Bill Brewer had chosen a restaurant in the hills with a view of city lights tumbling down sloping ground to the harbor, where they were reflected in water. He was waiting at a table by a window when Tash arrived.

"Don't blame me for being late. Blame Barlovento. I got bogged down in their imports and exports again and forgot the time."

"Campari soda?"

"Something stronger tonight, please. Rum, I think."

Bill ordered a daiquiri. "You look worried."

"I am."

"Want to talk about it?"

Tash took a sip of the cold, bitter-sweet drink and smiled over the rim of her glass at Bill. "I like talking to you. I can say anything that comes into my head without worrying for fear you'll misunderstand. I really need that tonight, but there mustn't be any leaks."

Bill laughed. "Have you forgotten that our paper is owned by a man who is supporting Playfair for re-election? No matter what you tell me tonight, I can't publish it."

"Censorship?"

"Of course. In a Freudian society, freedom of the press means freedom to print four-letter words, but you can't print the truth about international oil. Sex is the new opiate of the people."

"Don't you believe in anything? Not even sex?"

"Oh, I believe in dry martinis and you. What's this all about?"

Tash told him.

"I wonder if any love story ever has a happy ending," he said. "I remember so well when Jeremy married Vivian. He was really in love with her then."

"There must be some happy endings."

"I've never known one in real life. I loved my wife and what happened? She died of cancer before she was thirty . . .

"This is Jeremy Playfair's unlucky year, saddled with a wife whose behavior could wreck him, and stuck with a strike he can't settle without antagonizing some block of voters. Is it really bad luck? Or could it be the work of someone out to get him?"

"Oh, Bill, what a horrid idea! Do you think Hilary's right about Vivian Playfair?"

"It's possible, but not probable."

"Why not?"

"Alcoholism is escape. What has Mrs. Playfair to escape from?"

"An exhibitionist would love being a governor's wife," said Tash. "But a reticent person might find it torture after a year or so."

"Or she might fall in love with another man," said Bill. "How about Carlos de Miranda?"

"That's lunacy!" retorted Tash. "Do you think any woman married to Jeremy Playfair would look at any other man?"

Bill didn't try to return that ball. Apparently, he decided that it was not in his court.

They had reached coffee and liqueurs when he was called to the telephone.

Tash saw a change in him when he came back.

"I'm going to put you in a taxi now," he said. "I have to get back to the office."

"What's happened?"

"A clash between dockworkers and Barloventan exiles on the waterfront a few minutes ago. Two men killed, more than a dozen wounded."

When Tash reached Leafy Way with her suitcases she was waylaid by Hilary at the front door.

"We need you."

"But it's nearly midnight!"

"Did you think I was joking when I said we work twenty-four hours a day?"

In the Florida Room, the air was thick with tobacco smoke. Job Jackman stood where Carlos had stood the night before, his back to the fireplace, smoking the inevitable cigar. Jeremy sat negligently perched on the edge of a window seat. Carlos, arms folded, stood leaning his back against a table.

In a crisis Job was a different man from the one Tash had met two days ago. Even his voice had more authority now.

" . . . and now you must get the strike settled."

"Agreed," said Jeremy.

"Well, what are you waiting for? Give the strikers whatever they want."

"Disagreed."

Job took the cigar out of his mouth and flicked away the ash.

"Jeremy, being called neo-fascist and pro-Communist

88

at the same time is quite a feat, but that's what's happening to you now in the evening papers. If you call out the National Guard, it'll be even worse. You're not running for re-election in Barlovento. Why do you care if people there starve a little?"

"I've already called out the National Guard."

"Without consulting me?"

"There is no law or precedent that says I have to consult you."

"Do you know why you've never lost an election? Because I've managed all your campaigns."

"This isn't campaign strategy. This is state policy."

"Are you going to be like the President who said to his campaign manager: 'Mr. Tweed, God elected me!' "

"Job, I am not going to turn myself into a robot who jumps through hoops every time you push a button marked *Votes*. It's not the end of the world if I lose this election. Right now, I'm pretty sick of the whole thing. Carlos, doesn't your family still have a place on one of the islands where I could retire?"

"Cayo Siesta in the Sotavento group. Casa Miranda is yours, Jerry, whenever you care to go there."

"But the election!" It was almost a wail from Job. "Think of all the people who've worked for you without pay ever since you entered politics! Can you let them down by walking out in a moment of pique?"

"Pique?"

"Sorry, maybe that's the wrong word, but—"

"That is the wrong word. Two men have died, others have been wounded, because I listened to you too long and did not call out the National Guard. What I feel now can scarcely be described as pique."

"What are you going to do now?" Job's voice was chastened, almost meek.

"Tell the strikers at the meeting tomorrow that if they

89

will not accept the new terms, I shall ask the courts for an injunction against the strike."

It was the first time Tash had slept at Leafy Way. Perhaps it was the brightness of the moon, shining through an uncurtained window which she had left open for air that woke her in the middle of the night.

When she couldn't get back to sleep, she went over to the window and stepped out on a balcony there. It was hardly a working balcony, just an architect's whim, only about two feet wide.

She stood looking across a lawn blanched by moonlight to a belt of trees, then glanced down at the stone terrace below the balcony.

It was a shock to find herself looking down directly into another human face that was looking up at her.

She had not heard a sound. The moment was so still that her first thought was: hallucination.

For this was a face that had haunted her memory for a long time: pale eyes, blurred and blind-looking, the elfin smile of of a fallen angel.

For an instant, neither he nor she moved or spoke. The shock of mutual discovery cast a spell over both of them.

Then, still soundless, he melted across the grass into the trees.

She went through the motions of calling the guard room on her bedside telephone. She was not surprised when Captain Wilkes called back an hour later to say that his men had not been able to find anyone in the grounds.

9

NEXT MORNING, the executive offices were as grimly busy as a command post on the edge of a combat zone.

Everyone knew that violence on the waterfront was now held in check only by the presence of national guardsmen.

At twelve noon the Governor went to the State House to meet representatives of all three parties—the strikers and the Barloventan immigrants and Barloventan political exiles—in a last effort to patch up some sort of truce that would at least avoid further bloodshed.

Carlos went with him as interpreter. Job remained at Leafy Way with Tash, putting together the rough draft of a statement which the Governor was to make on television at seven o'clock that evening.

Whether a truce was established or not, he wanted to make a short, clear statement of the issues so that the electorate would know what was going on while it was going on.

The executive offices were in such turmoil that Job and Tash went to work in Jeremy's own office on the floor above, the Octagonal Room, a tower room with a view of the garden on all eight sides.

It was the first time Tash had worked with Job, and

she found him less easy to work with than anyone else in the Tennis Cabinet. The little courtesies that lubricate social mechanisms were neglected by Job. Perhaps they were incompatible with the Boss Tweed role he wanted to play in politics. That populist tradition demanded sand in the machine, not oil.

All morning Tash had an uncomfortable feeling of gears clashing, gritty surfaces grinding together, and abrasive metals uttering high-pitched squeals.

What Jeremy or Carlos would have conveyed as a smiling request, Job growled as a surly command, while the series of cigars in his mouth made the atmosphere almost unbreathable by one o'clock.

Yet it was impossible to work with him without recognizing one thing: his single-minded devotion to Jeremy's service. Job had what Bill Brewer called a fundamentalist mind. He would never be troubled by self-doubt, or by doubt of any chief to whom he had given allegiance.

When he had cut Tash's first rough draft from thirty pages to twenty, it was better. When he had cut the twenty-page version to fifteen pages, it was still better.

He lit a cigar complacently. "Have you any suggestions now?"

"Yes. I would cut three more pages and reduce the total to twelve instead of fifteen."

"Which paragraphs would you cut?"

"I wouldn't cut by paragraph. I'd cut by line. We have fifteen pages of twenty-five lines each. I would cut five lines from each page. That's a total of seventy-five lines or three pages."

"And it would still make sense?"

"More sense than before. Cutting by paragraph is butchery, but cutting by line is surgery. There's hardly any blood. Almost like cutting a callus off your heel."

"Where did you learn this?"

"Working for newspapers and magazines that would cut anything to the bone to make room for a four-line ad."

"Let's see you cut this."

Tash went through the script with a soft-leaded pencil as swiftly as if she were making merely typographical corrections.

Job took it from her and read.

"Well, I'll be damned!" It was the mildest of his colloquial expressions. "If Jeremy retires, will you write speeches for me?"

"Maybe. Shall I have this typed now?"

"Yes, and tell the secretariat to make a dozen Xeroxes and put them on Jeremy's desk in this room."

A tap on the door.

"Sorry." It was Hilary's voice. "You'll have to get out now. The TV men are here to set up their equipment."

"Let's go and have a snack in the mess," said Job to Tash.

Outside, the corridor seemed narrower now it was choked with an unseemly clutter of cables, monitors, strobe light fixtures, throat microphones, and other mysteries which men from a network were dragging into the Octagonal Room.

In the mess hall, Job planked a pocket radio on the table beside his cup of coffee and tuned in a local station that was hitched to one of the national networks.

". . . according to a reliable source, strikers and immigrants have both made concessions to compromise, but the Barloventan political exiles are refusing to yield an inch. This afternoon, the Orioles . . ."

Job switched off his radio.

"Damn those expatriates!" He pronounced it as if it were spelled "expatriot."

"I thought you were for them last night."

93

"I'm not for them or against them. I don't give one ice-cube in hell about them or their lousy island. All I care about is the Governor's future."

A girl from the secretariat brought them two copies of the Xeroxed statement.

As Tash read, she herself was now surprised to see how her Barloventan researches that had taken her so many hours of tedious work were now reduced to a few brisk sentences without losing anything essential.

Job looked up from the text. "Well?"

Tash spoke cautiously. "I think it's quite good."

"Good? It's terrific! The delivery time is right, too. It takes Jerry about two minutes to read a page of twenty-five lines aloud, so twelve pages will take him about twenty-four minutes."

"Is he going to read this?"

"Yes, but the television audience won't know it. He'll have the script on the desk in front of him, below the camera, where the audience can't see it, but he can glance down at it whenever he wants to. He's practised that until it looks as if he wasn't reading at all."

"Do you think this will change opinion in the legislature?"

"Probably not. A good speech will change a politician's mind, but not his vote. We're aiming to change voters' opinions. Then the legislators will have to follow suit, or lose votes." Job looked at his watch. "Nearly seven. Want to go up to the Octagonal Room or shall we watch here?"

"Wouldn't we just be in the way up there?"

"Probably."

"Then let's watch it here."

Men and women from research and secretariat were drifting into the mess hall to hear the speech. Job went to the TV set and turned knobs until there was a flash of the state flag on screen and a voice from off screen intoned:

"His Excellency, the Governor of—"

Burst of static.

Job swore and fiddled with the volume button. Tash remembered that only two other states in the Union—Massachusetts and New Hampshire—still used a form of address inherited from colonial governors: Your Excellency.

Jeremy's face came on screen. He looked tired, but there was still the irrepressible glint in his eyes that seemed to say: *I refuse to take anything in this cockeyed world seriously.*

He was upstairs in the Octagonal Room sitting at his own desk, which someone had stripped of its usual clutter.

Tash felt like a split personality as she listened to her own words in this other voice, clear, strong, masculine. Every time the small audience laughed or clapped she felt a surge of pride.

Job seemed to have the same feeling. "No last minute changes so far," he whispered. "You and I did a good job." He looked at his wristwatch. "Twenty-two and a half minutes gone and half a page to go. Right on the nose."

He touched his finger to his own nose in the immemorial radio-television gesture, and then gasped: "Oops! What's up?"

The camera had not shifted, but Carlos had stepped into its view on screen. He stood behind Jeremy's chair, a little to Jeremy's right. He looked the ideal aide-de-camp, deferential but self-respecting, as he leaned forward to slide a piece of paper into Jeremy's right hand.

Carlos stepped back. Once more Jeremy was alone on

95

screen. He glanced down at the paper, then lifted his eyes with a smile.

It was not a political smile, muscular and self-conscious. It was a spontaneous, almost boyish grin which made it hard to realize he was smiling at an audience he could not see. There was real joy in his voice as he ignored the last page of his script and improvised his final words.

"And now I must ask you to excuse me. I have important things to do. The strike has been settled."

Another flash of the state flag on screen blotted out his face and there was a burst of martial music. No one paid any attention to the music or to the news commentator's voice that followed it. Everyone in the room was clapping and crowding around Job, the only member of the state government present.

As soon as he could get away, he and Tash hurried upstairs.

"Jeremy has a sense of the dramatic," she said.

"You're a dead duck if you don't," retorted Job. "Of course that dirty rag, the *Morning Globe*, will try to make it sound as if Jeremy knew all about this settlement before he went on the air and arranged for Carlos to pass him that note to make the announcement dramatic, but you and I know that isn't true. Jeremy doesn't plan things. They just happen to him because he has luck, and then, naturally, he always rises to the occasion."

By the time they got up to the Octagonal Room, Jeremy had left with Carlos for a final meeting with the Barloventan exiles, who were now accusing him of "betraying" them by settling the strike.

Hilary took them down to the Florida Room to wait for Jeremy.

"I want to tell him that Vivian was delighted with the the speech," she said.

"Isn't she sitting up for him?" asked Job.

"No. She must get to sleep early. Doctor's orders."

It was after ten when Jeremy and Carlos arrived. Then there were drinks and cold meats and salads, congratulations and post-mortems and projections of the future.

It isn't a party, thought Tash. It's the celebration of a clan victory.

For the first time she realized that the people to whom you become attached in life are not those with whom you share pleasure, but those with whom you share work and pain, risk and responsibility.

At midnight Jeremy said: "I think it's time we broke this up. Hilary, thank you for all you've done." He kissed her lightly and sexlessly on one cheek. "And thank you, too, Tash." He kissed her cheek just as lightly, just as sexlessly. "Good night. *Sogni d'oro!*"

Upstairs, Tash and Hilary parted company at Hilary's door and Tash went on down the corridor to her own rooms.

Inside, she closed the door, but she did not turn on a light. She went out on the balcony and knelt down; folding her arms on the railing and resting a cheek on one arm, she looked up at a bright, white glaze of stars.

So this was the "reason" she had taken the job at Leafy Way. This was why she had told Bill Brewer it was "something she had to do." Even then she was already in love with Jeremy in the timeless, unmoral depths of being far below the social self.

She had told herself she would never fall in love, as if it were something she could control. She should have remembered that it is dangerous to insult Aphrodite, who always takes her revenge on those who defy her power, men or women.

Casual kissing had started in the theatre world and spread finally to the respectable suburbs. Nine times out of ten it meant nothing to the man or the woman, but there was always that tenth time when it might mean something to one of them.

Only to one? Could such strong feeling exist without being reciprocated at all?

If only he hadn't kissed her she might never have known the truth about herself.

She had a liking for Vivian Playfair and, more than liking, compassion, now she knew Vivian was in some kind of trouble. Whatever that trouble was, a divorce, however discreet, would spread it all over the front page of every newspaper in the country and the world.

Even the most carefully managed love affair was hardly an asset in politics. A divorce could be disaster.

She remembered years ago hearing an old man say to a young man: "What should you do if you find yourself falling in love with a married woman? Run like hell!"

Some people pretended that infidelity and divorce did not involve emotions or morals. She knew better. She could remember the unhappiness in her father's voice when he said to her mother: *I didn't want this to happen. Try to think of me as if I had been driving a rickety car too fast on a rough mountain road. . . .*

If you had time to jump out of a car before it crashed, you jumped.

Tomorrow she would hand in her resignation.

10

WHICH IS WORSE, to have nature mock unhappiness with a sunny day, or match it with clouds and rain?

When Tash awoke, rain was whipping the windowpanes and the dull sky seemed close enough to touch.

She moved heavily, as if her hands and feet were weighted with lead. She dressed without self-awareness, a computer going through a programmed routine.

It was so early, the mess hall was empty when she got downstairs. She looked at the scrambled eggs in the chafing-dish with distaste and drank a cup of black coffee.

In her own office the daylight was so thin that she had to switch on a lamp beside her typewriter.

She began to type.

Dear Jeremy,
To my deep regret I find that I must offer you my resignation to take effect as soon as possible. The strain of working so late . . .

She exxed out the last sentence. He knew irregular hours meant nothing to a newspaper woman.

She tried again:

I am resigning for purely personal reasons . . .

Such as what?

She could say she had to be with her mother in Boston or her father in Rome. Neither of them would deny it, but what a shabby lie!

She could remember her father quoting Amiel's *Journal: Every lie must be paid for. Truth always takes her revenge.* . . .

I'm getting married. To whom?

I don't like the job. He would know that wasn't true.

She remembered her mother saying that if you must decline an invitation there are only two excuses that will not hurt people's feelings: either you have another engagement or you are ill. As everyone knew, this was a convention, not a lie but a formula for saving face.

She could not bring herself to malingering, but couldn't she suggest she had another engagement? In this context, another job?

It was too early for the editor of a morning newspaper to be at his office, but Bill Brewer's home number was in the telephone book.

She dialed and listened to the bell drilling the silence with its nagging, repetitive peal. She couldn't visualize the place where it was ringing, for she had never been to Bill's house.

A sleepy voice mumbled in her ear. "H'lo?"

"Bill?"

"Why, Tash!" The voice was wide awake.

"I'm sorry I woke you."

"It doesn't matter."

"It would matter if this wasn't a kind of crisis."

"What kind of crisis?"

"Let's say a small crisis. I want to give up this job, but I must have a reasonably plausible excuse for doing so.

Would you be willing to say you need me back on the paper again?"

Bill laughed. "Of course. And it's true. I do need you."

"Oh, Bill, how can I thank you?"

"Are you going to tell me your real reason for resigning?"

"Some day, perhaps, but now now, and not over the telephone."

"Tash, are you in trouble of any kind?"

"Only trouble of my own making. Nobody knows about it except me. You know the worst things in life don't happen out in the world around us. They happen inside our own skulls. If you can keep that in mind, you can keep things in proportion."

"When are you coming back to work?"

"As soon as I can. I'll let you know after I've talked to Jerry."

"Jerry?"

"Jeremy, Governor Playfair."

"Oh, I see. Well, call me as soon as you can. I'll be in the office by noon."

"Thank you, Bill. Good-bye."

Tash went back to her typewriter:

. . . to take effect as soon as possible. William Brewer, the editor of . . .

She sat back looking at her unfinished letter. Then she wrenched it out of the typewriter, crumpled it into a ball, and hurled the ball into her scrapbasket.

She picked up the telephone again and dialed the switchboard.

"Nick, do you know where the Governor is now?"

"In the Octagonal Room."

"Is he awfully busy?"

101

"I don't know. Mr. de Miranda is with him."

"Will you ring the number for me, please?"

Carlos answered.

"This is Tash. I'd like to talk to the Governor this morning. Can you suggest a good time?"

"Hold on a moment."

She heard a rumble of voices in the background, then Carlos spoke again. "Why don't you come now? It's as good a time as any."

On the stairs she was aware of her own heart beats, not quicker but heavier, and so loud she was afraid other people would hear them. Yet it had to be this way. She couldn't resign by letter after being with Jeremy so much the last few days. He would think it odd. He might even suspect a hidden motive. She must try to be natural, casual, and nonchalant.

Carlos met her at the door. "Jerry's giving you ten minutes. A great honor because he's really busy."

That made it all the worse.

"Will ten minutes be enough?"

"It should be."

"While you're talking to him, I'll be working on the timetable of his Western trip. Don't take more than ten minutes. Every second counts from now till polling day."

Jeremy was standing in the tall, bay window at the far end of the eight-sided room, looking out at the rain, slashing the windowpanes. He turned and smiled.

"Good morning, Tash. Nothing wrong, I hope?"

"Not really." Her throat was dry. She had to swallow. Her hands were shaky. Her knees just weren't there.

"I don't quite know how to say this. I'm really sorry, but . . ."

"But what?"

"I've come to . . . well, resign."

The ghost at the back of her mind asked her if is this

102

was her idea of being natural, casual, and nonchalant?

Jeremy had been in public life too long for his expression to betray his inner feelings. His manner was pleasantly polite and totally unreadable.

"My dear Tash, why?"

"Oh, didn't I say? It's Bill Brewer, my editor. He wants be back on the newspaper. He says he really needs me."

"I need you, too. It's only a few months till the election. Couldn't Mr. Brewer possibly spare you for that short time?"

"I'm afraid not."

"I was depending on you."

"I know. That's what makes me feel so badly about it."

"Would it do any good if I talked to Brewer?"

"I don't think so."

Jeremy smiled suddenly. "Would it do any good if I talked to you?"

She was speechless. She could only shake her head.

"Have you given me the real reason for your resignation? Or has something happened to make you unhappy here?"

"Oh, it's nothing like that. I have been happy here. It's just that I . . . well, I owe it to Bill. He gave me my first job when I first came to this state and I can't let him down."

"If that's the way you feel, there's not much I can say, but wouldn't you like to think it over for a few days or a week?"

"No, thanks. That wouldn't make any difference. It's better to do this quickly. I'll just stay until you can get someone else."

"That won't be necessary." There was a touch of coldness in his voice. "We can find someone else in a day or so. And now, if you will excuse me?"

He sat down at his desk and began studying the papers

that lay on the blotter. Without looking up he said: "When you get back to the executive offices, please tell Carlos I'm ready for him now."

As she went out, she looked at a clock. It had taken only three minutes.

She ought to have been happy because she had done the right thing, but now she discovered as many have before her that doing the right thing does not necessarily make you happy. She had done what she had always believed her father should have done fourteen years ago, and the result was that she had never felt more unhappy in her life. For the first time she began to understand what her father had gone through. He had acted as he had to escape a desolation like that she felt now.

If her resignation had been announced on television, it could not have flashed through the executive offices more instantaneously.

Carlos was the first to approach her, angry and plaintive at the same time. He said all the things Jeremy might have said and didn't. How could she let the Governor down? How could she leave now, of all times, on the very eve of a campaign? Who was going to write the speeches for the Governor's western trip? Did she think he, Carlos, could carry the whole burden alone? Why had she taken on this job if she didn't mean to keep it until after the election? Her leaving at such short notice was a disgrace to her and an insult to the Governor. Didn't she have any sense of loyalty at all?

Tash was far more able to face this storm than Jeremy's coldness.

"I'm sorry, but my job is not that important to you or to the Governor. And I did offer to wait until he could get someone else."

Carlos left her office, still fuming, and Job arrived.

"Another county heard from!" He was quoting the oft

104

repeated cry of the men who kept tally at party head-quarters when election returns were coming in. "I'm surprised at you."

"Job, I'm tired of apologizing. I know it must seem awful to you who have been with Jeremy so long, but—"

"But you have to think of yourself."

"And Bill Brewer and the newspaper."

"Boloney. That's not your real reason."

It was hard to meet those sharp eyes. She was more afraid of Job's shrewdness than of Jeremy's disdain or Carlos' indignation.

Job removed the cigar from his mouth, always a signal that he was going to say something of importance.

"Jerry's election means everything to me, and I think you're the one for this job, much better than your prede-cessor was. Not everyone can work smoothly with Car-los and Hilary. Not everyone has your knack with words. There's hardly time to find anyone else as good as you. Will you stay if I see to it your salary is doubled, starting today?"

"It's not a question of money."

"Yeah? Job gave her a hard look. "Everything is a question of money . . . or sex. What else is there?"

"Children and . . ."

"And honor? Don't say it. Even you couldn't be that naïve. Think about my offer for the next twenty-four hours. Let me know tomorrow."

He was gone before she could answer.

She fell briskly to work tidying up her desk, hoping drudgery would take her mind off other things. It didn't.

She knew now that Job, least sensitive member of the Tennis Cabinet, was the only one who suspected the truth at all. She was afraid of his giving her away to the others. He would if he had anything to gain by it.

Better go the first thing in the morning without seeing

him or anyone else again. She could leave a note for him on his desk refusing his offer.

Her own desk was now piled high with a mass of data on the western counties, which research had just sent over for her to use in Jeremy's western speeches. All she could do about that was to spend her last day reducing the incoherent mass to a working brief for her successor.

By the time she finished that, a gleam of watery sunshine was leaking through the clouds. The rain had ceased. The only sound now was the steady dripping of a drainpipe.

She looked up at the sky and saw the traditional patch of blue big enough to make a Dutchman's breeches. When she raised the window, a moist, earthy, almost tropical smell came in from the garden. The rain had not brought coolness.

She was closing her typewriter when Hilary arrived.

"Don't say it," said Tash. "You're furious because I am resigning, and you want me to reconsider, but I won't."

"That isn't what I came to say." Hilary sat down and stretched out her legs as if her muscles were cramped. "However, since you've brought it up yourself, why are you resigning?"

"Bill Brewer wants me back."

"That badly?"

Tash nodded.

"And you feel your obligation to him is more important than your obligation to Jeremy?"

"Yes. I'm sorry."

Hilary took a moment to light a cigarette, then looked up without smiling and said: "I think you're a fool."

"What did you come to say to me?"

"Vivian is leaving early tomorrow morning for the nursing home. She would like to say good-bye to you before she goes."

"Now?"

"As soon as you're ready."

"Does she know I'm leaving?"

"No, and there's no need to tell her. It might upset her."

"I don't see why my going should upset her."

"Everybody thinks your going is peculiar because no one believes the reason you give for doing so."

"Does she know the canary is dead?"

"No one has told her. We've been told to shield her from anything that might disturb her. Jeremy hasn't even questioned her about that letter she asked you to mail."

They climbed the stairs together, Tash thinking: I shall never go upstairs in this house again.

"We ought to have elevators," said Hilary.

"Oh, no, the stairway is so beautiful!"

"That's what Jeremy says, but if he had to go up and down as often as the rest of us—"

"Don't tell me you're criticizing Jeremy!"

That brought a spark to Hilary's eyes. "I do frequently. Didn't you know?"

At the door Hilary tapped gently and a voice said: "Come in!"

Juana opened the door and stood aside to let them enter.

The curtains were drawn back now, and Tash saw the room clearly for the first time. Thin, after-rain sunlight flooded the *boiserie*, painted lavender-gray, and the tall, taffeta curtains of a harmonious mauve. Rugs and furniture were old and faded and French. The only dark note in the pale room was a Chinese screen that protected the bed from draughts, black lacquer inlaid with mother-of-pearl.

Vivian's eyes followed Tash's glance around the room.

107

"That paneling hasn't been repainted since the eighteenth century. You only get housekeeping like that in official residences."

This room doesn't express her, thought Tash. She has let her role as governor's wife smother her real self.

For all its grace, the room was obviously a sickroom now. The astringence of lavender smelling salts hovered in the air. A glass of fruit juice stood on the bedside table; beside it, a small bottle with a typewritten label: *Mrs. J. Playfair Two at bedtime as directed. Dr. Clemens. # 104623.*

Yet Vivian did not look sick. There was no longer a dressing on her temple. The bruise had faded and the cut had healed. Her pallor was no more than the pallor of anyone who has been kept indoors.

"Smoke?" She held out a cigarette case. "Oh, I forgot! You don't." She lit a cigarette for herself, dropping the burnt match into a Sévres ashtray almost hidden in a fold of frilly counterpane.

"You're still doing it," said Tash.

"What? Oh, the ashtray on the bed."

"Please don't. It is dangerous."

"It really bothers you, doesn't it?" Vivian smiled. "All right. Since it worries you that much, I promise to keep the ashtray on the table."

"Starting now." Tash put the ashtray on the bedside table.

Juana stared at this performance in astonishment.

Tash tried to explain to her in lame, phrasebook Spanish: *"El cenicero siempre en la mesa, por favor; no en la cama. Es peligroso. Fuego."*

Juana smiled shyly and nodded her head as if she understood. That smile on that mutilated face was the most pathetic thing Tash had ever seen. Never again would she think of Juana as grotesque.

"Don't worry about it," said Vivian. "I have my faults,

but I keep my promises. Now do sit down."

Tash pulled up a small chair to the bedside. "I'm sorry you're going away. Everyone here is going to miss you."

"Thanks, but I don't expect to be missed."

Hilary started to protest.

Vivian stilled her with a look. "For one thing, I won't be gone that long. It's just a check-up. I may even be back in time to go on this campaign trip with Jerry. I'd like that. The west is the most fascinating part of this state. Impenetrable dialect, archaic schools, fundamentalist churches, but fascinating folklore, the best hunting and fishing we have, and the fieriest white mule, distilled illegally, of course. There's a kind of lazy, lawless, fey charm about those people you don't find anywhere else. If only Jerry and I could go there alone, just the two of us."

"You know that's not possible in an election year," said Hilary.

"I know only too well." Vivian reached for the ashtray, stubbed out her cigarette, and put the ashtray back on the table. "See?" She smiled at Tash. "I won't forget. What I really wanted to say to you is that I'm sorry I've seen so little of you since you came here. I hope we can make up for that when I come back."

On the stairs once more, Tash looked at Hilary. "She didn't say anything about her loss of memory."

"She never mentions it. She behaves as if it had never happened."

"Do you think she really has no memory of anything that happened while she was away?"

"I think she's forgotten because she wants to forget. Can you think of any better reason for letting sleeping dogs lie? I've always thanked God that memory is selective. Life couldn't go on if we had to remember everything."

"That's heresy to the modern psychiatrist."

"And look at the mess he's made of the human mind in less than a hundred years. Nature is wiser than we are. Blotting out an intolerable memory is a survival trait, like growing scar tissue. I just hope this new doctor knows what he's doing."

"Why did she change doctors?"

"The other one, Dr. Grant, didn't seem to be doing her any good, so Jeremy called in his own doctor, Henry Clemens. Now if she could just get rid of that gargoyle of a maid—"

"Is that how you think of Juana?"

"Don't you?"

"Not now that I've talked to her and seen her smile."

They had come to the door of Tash's office.

"Hilary, when Vivian comes back and finds I'm gone, please tell her I'm sorry I had to go without saying good-bye. In other circumstances, she and I could have been friends."

"When are you going?"

"Tomorrow morning early."

"Then I'll say good-bye now." Hilary held out her hand. "We must have luncheon together in town once you're settled back in your old job."

She was the only person who had spoken of wanting to see Tash again.

It took only a few moments to pack personal possessions in a brief case. She took it and her portable typewriter with her when she went into the mess hall for something to eat.

It was early for supper. Two women from the secretariat were at the far end of the room drinking tea, but there was no one else in sight.

Tash played with a salad for a while, then went upstairs to her own rooms, stopping at the guard room on her way to surrender her office key to the man on duty.

Her two suitcases were in the closet. She packed swiftly, took a cold shower, and put on the thinnest nightgown that came to hand. It happened to be filmy white with a matching robe, the sort of thing our grandmothers called a negligée.

She pulled a long chair over to a French window that was standing open on the balcony. Half-sitting, half-reclining she could see the last daylight draining from the pale, rain-washed sky.

She tried to read. By the time the first star came out, she had put the book down. She didn't feel hungry. She felt empty. How was she ever going to get to sleep tonight?

At last she remembered a bottle of rum Carlos had given her to keep in her rooms when she first moved into Leafy Way. "For dire emergency," he had said. "Such as the bar being closed."

It was still standing, unopened, on the hat shelf in her clothes closet.

She opened it now. There was always fresh ice-water in the Thermos jug beside her bed. She filled a glass and took it back to the long chair in the sitting room.

The stars came out one by one to watch and keep her company while she sipped her drink. The empty feeling began to melt away. Physically she felt looser, mentally she felt enlarged. Now she could say with true faith: *This, too, will pass.*

She looked at the clock. Nearly eleven. One more drink, a smaller one, and she would sleep, and leave early tomorrow morning and put the whole thing behind her forever.

She was only twenty-five. The greater part of life was still ahead of her.

She heard the light knock, but didn't pay attention to it until it came a second time.

Hilary? So late?

She went to the door and threw it open.

On the threshold stood Jeremy Playfair.

11

"I HAD TO talk to you. I knew you were awake because I saw your light."

His voice was almost inaudible. Never before had she seen him so subdued.

"Come in," she said, and shut the door as he stepped inside. "I was just having a drink. Would you like one?"

"Thanks, I need one."

He must have been playing tennis earlier that evening, for he was wearing sneakers, slacks, and a tennis shirt.

"Has something happened?"

He hesitated over his answer. "A lot of things have happened, including your resignation. Why did you resign?"

"But I told you, the newspaper—"

"Please. Let's have the truth."

Had she been telling the truth all along, she would have protested indignantly. But she had been suppressing the true and suggesting the false, which is lying, no matter what the Supreme Court says, so she hesitated.

That moment's hesitation gave him an advantage. He seized it quickly. "You don't defend yourself because you know you can't. Now tell me the real reason you resigned."

"Is there any rule that says one has to give a reason?"

"No rule, but it is customary."

"I gave you enough reason to satisfy custom."

He moved his glass, swirling the drink in a miniature whirlpool. "You gave no reason. Just a transparently false excuse. Mr. Brewer and his newspaper can get along without you perfectly well and you know it."

"You've been making inquiries?"

"Of course. I questioned that reporter of his who covers the State House. You are not needed on the paper now any more than you were when you gave up the job to come here. So what is your real reason?"

"I'm not going to tell you. Let's just leave it at that."

Tash expected him to finish his drink and walk out of the room, but he didn't. He sat quietly looking through the open window at the arch of stars above the dark treetops. At last he spoke.

"Is it because of something you found out?"

"I don't know what you mean."

"I am asking you if you found out the truth about Vivian."

Until now it had all seemed a simple matter of an employer irritated because he was losing an employee at an inconvenient moment. Even this unconventional visit to her rooms late at night was just the informal Playfair charm being used to paper over a crack in staff organization.

Now she saw that it must be more than that.

"All I know about Vivian is what you and others have told me."

He looked at her steadily. "I'm not sure I believe you."

"There's only one thing I know about her that you may not know."

"And that is?"

"The first time I saw her here she asked me to mail a

letter for her, and the letter was stolen before I could mail it, but that has nothing to do with my resignation."

"Tell me all about the letter."

He listened without any sign of surprise.

"And even then it didn't occur to you what was wrong?"

"No."

"Then I think I shall have to tell you."

"I'd rather you didn't. I might let it slip to someone else without meaning to."

"No. You wouldn't."

"But why tell me at all?"

"I have to protect Vivian. The mystery about her must be the reason for your resignation. What else could there be? Since you already know enough to suspect her, you might as well know the whole truth. Then you may feel less like resigning.

"Suppose I let you go without another word, what happens? I have to get someone else, someone who is sure to suspect something is wrong with Vivian just as you did, but who may be so much less understanding than you that I could never confide in him or her as I am confiding in you now. Don't you see how much more difficult everything would be for me then?"

"I don't want to make things difficult for you. What is it you want to tell me?"

"Like everything else that seems complex when you don't know what it's about, this is really simple when you do. It can be expressed in five or six words."

He lifted his eyes and looked her full in the face. "Vivian takes drugs. Hard drugs."

Everything fell into place.

The sudden change in Vivian's spirits and appearance? A common symptom of cocaine addiction. Her loss of memory? Partial amnesia was another symptom associated with several drugs. The nursing home where she was going tomorrow? A clinic for the cure of addicts where Jeremy was sending her now he knew the truth. The absence of children in her marriage? Some drugs were said to affect fertility, especially when more than one was taken at a time.

The letter smuggled out of Leafy Way through Tash herself? An attempt to communicate secretly with a drug supplier. She couldn't send or receive many letters on her own without drawing attention to what she was doing. All her personal mail, incoming and outgoing, was filtered through the office of her social secretary, Hilary. If she bypassed that office more than once or twice, Hilary would want to know why.

She couldn't use the telephone at Leafy Way for such purposes. There were a dozen lines, but they all went through the switchboard manned by operators from the state police guard.

Her periodic disappearances without her own car? Times when she had to make contact with a drug supplier in person. She couldn't go just anywhere in her own car. Its license number was known to every policeman in the state, and her face was known to every reader of news magazines. She couldn't take a taxi. A driver who recognized her might talk. A driver who suspected her might blackmail her.

Any contacts with a drug supplier she had to make in person would have to be made alone and after dark, slipping out a French window, walking down the neglected right of way to the nearest public transportation.

If she wanted to stay away for several days, there would be no search for her as long as she telephoned Jeremy or Hilary that she was staying with friends. If any reporters asked Jeremy about her mysterious disappearances, he would in all good faith, deny there was any mystery about her absences.

All these things were commonplaces of drug addiction. Only one thing made Vivian's case uncommon: She was the wife of the governor of the state.

"She must have felt Hilary was more like a jailer than a social secretary," said Tash.

"Guards can become jailers overnight," responded Jeremy. "It all depends on your point of view."

"How long have you known?"

"Only since that night she came home alone in her car, almost unconscious. I sent for my own doctor and he told me what was wrong. Do you think I would have announced my candidacy at the dinner that very night if I had known what was going on? Until then I thought she was going through some kind of mental illness. I kept trying to get her to see a psychiatrist, but she wouldn't. How could she? He would have seen what was wrong immediately."

Tash remembered his concern for her. *Viv, are you sure you're not overdoing things? . . . Take care of yourself, Viv. Promise. . . .*

"Now I understand why my resignation made you angry. It must have seemed like desertion."

"Not angry." He smiled with rue. "Just scared. I was afraid you had discovered the truth, and I didn't know what you might do about it after you left. So tonight I decided to tell you everything. I'm asking you to keep her secret until she can be cured."

"You don't have to ask. Of course I'll do everything I can. Did you think of going to the police for help?"

"You've heard Wilkes on addicts. Would you turn an addict you cared about over to him? This is a matter for doctors, not police."

"Is this one reason your new anti-drug law is more merciful to addicts than pushers?"

"I signed that bill before I knew about Vivian, but how can I make anyone believe that I didn't know? Can

117

you imagine how the press would crucify me if they discovered now that my own wife was an addict?"

"It's a perfect set up for blackmail."

"Yes, isn't it? I thought of that. So far there have been no attempts."

"How many people know now, besides you and the doctor?"

"Only Hilary and Carlos. I told them because I needed their help, and they were likely to find out anyway, living in such close relations with Vivian and me. Luckily, Hilary is an old friend of my mother's family and Carlos has been my closest friend since Princeton. They won't talk."

"What about Vivian's maid, Juana?"

"I doubt if such a thing would occur to her. She's good at manual jobs, but she's not intelligent. Even in her own language she's illiterate, and she doesn't understand English."

"When did it begin?"

"I don't know when or how or why. But I do know that if Vivian does not come back from the nursing home cured, I'll have to get out of politics altogether."

"So you meant it when you told Job that you really didn't care whether you ran for a second term or not?"

"I meant it all right, but I doubt if Job believed me. How could he when he doesn't know about Vivian?"

Jeremy's voice was steady, but there was naked pain in his eyes as he went on. "Tash, you must understand that I still love Vivian. So much so that I am tormented by the idea that this must have happened because I failed her in some way."

Tash couldn't leave him with that thought.

"Addiction is physical," she insisted. "Some people become addicts just because a careless doctor keeps them on pain-killing drugs too long during an illness. It

118

doesn't have to mean that Vivian was unhappy. It could be just that she fell among thieves."

"You mean among addicts?"

"That's how most new addicts are recruited. Vice loves company. It proselytes with the zeal of Victorian missionaries to the heathen."

"Of course. It must be a lonely business, being an outcast."

Jeremy walked over to the window and stood silent for a moment, looking up at the stars.

"Destroying Vivian is the perfect way to destroy me and everything I care about, my marriage and my career. I wonder if anyone hates me that much?"

"Isn't hate too strong a word?"

"You should see some of the hate letters that come into the mailroom here every day."

He began to pace the floor. "Why did I ever go into politics? I suppose it was because I like to gamble. This is the big game. Higher stakes than money."

Tash smiled. "You do like taking risks, don't you? Any other man would have got out of politics the moment he found out about Vivian. Another drink?"

"Yes, let's both have a nightcap and then I'll go. I feel a lot better than I did when I came into this room. I knew I had to tell you. For Vivian's sake I had to find out how much you knew. But I didn't want to tell you. I had no idea how you'd react."

So it had not occurred to him that she might be in love with him.

He stood, watching her add water to the drinks.

"You're still free to resign, if you still want to."

"Thanks." Tash curled up at the chair end of the chaise longue, sitting on her feet as she sipped her drink.

Jeremy sat on the long end below her. Glass in one hand, he reached out the other to clasp a hand of hers.

119

"Dear Tash, what do you really want to do now? Go or stay?"

"Stay."

There would be heartache in seeing him every day, knowing he loved Vivian, but there would be heartbreak in never seeing him again.

She disengaged her hand, brushing her hair back from her forehead to make the disengagement seem casual.

"What about the dead canary? Did anyone ever tell Vivian?"

"I told her the canary was dead, but I didn't tell her how he died."

"Did you know that I saw the boy pickpocket, Freaky, here in the grounds three nights ago?"

"Wilkes told me."

"I had an impression he was coming out of the house when I saw him. I've wondered about that. Could he get past the alarm system? Why did he and Halcòn steal Vivian's letter? How did they know I had her letter?"

"Wilkes is pretty good at his job, but even he can't answer those questions yet."

Jeremy put down his empty glass and looked at the clock.

"Good God! Three in the morning!" He laughed. "Anyone who sees me coming out of your rooms at this hour is going to get ideas."

He was halfway to the door when he paused to look back.

"Tash, I would have missed you if you'd gone. I like having you around."

That was the moment when the stillness of the night was shattered by the howl of a siren.

It went on and on and on, brazen-throated and inexhaustible, smashing against the eardrums and vibrating through all the dark, secret cavities of the body.

For a moment they could only stand and stare at one another.

Then Tash shouted above the racket: "What is it?"

"Fire."

"Here?"

"Must be. That's our alarm."

He opened the door.

They could not even see the corridor as great billows of smoke surged into the room.

12

Jeremy slammed the door. Curls of smoke seeped under the lintel and spiraled up toward the ceiling.

"Let's try the windows."

There was more than one siren shrieking now. It was pandemonium, a word to remind us that noise as well as fire is an ingredient of hell.

The first thing she saw from the window she never forgot—living trees on fire, blazing like giant torches with the brisk, crackling sound of a good fire on an open hearth, trees that had taken generations to grow. This place would not be Leafy Way again in her lifetime.

How often she had worked to coax green logs into a blaze. These logs weren't just green, they were alive, yet they needed no coaxing. They were burning as fast as paper, close to the house. This was not a "good" fire. This was the threat of death made visible.

"Where are the firemen?" she cried.

"On their way. Those sirens are theirs."

"And the first one?"

"Our alarm here in the house. It's supposed to be sensitive to both heat and smoke. I can't understand how the flames got such a start without its going off before."

"Can we jump or drop?"

Jeremy looked down at the terrace. "No. Especially

with flagstones below. We must wait for the firemen if we can."

They both turned to look at the door behind them. Now smoke was leaking through every crack, top, bottom, and sides.

"We may have to jump if they don't get here soon," said Jeremy. "Better a broken ankle than suffocation."

Now there were voices. A mob of people charged around the corner from the front of the house. They were running beside fire engines that had to move slowly over the turf.

Wilkes and two of his men were trying to block their way.

"Don't crowd the firemen. They know their job. You can't help."

There was the sound of an axe crashing through glass and wood. Just below the balcony, two firemen were trying to attach a hose to a standpipe. "Is there enough pressure?" asked somebody.

Water gushed. The firemen directed their jets toward windows nearer the front of the house where, as everyone knew, the Governor and his lady had their private apartments. Searchlights from fire engines were concentrating on that end, too. The balcony where Tash and Jeremy were standing was still in shadow. No one had noticed them yet.

Tash looked down at the crowd, now standing back a good way from the house. The only light that reached their upturned faces was a flicker of flame and shadow that jerked and leapt, pranced and pirouetted to the crackling music of burning trees.

It was hard not to think of that fire as something alive, hungry and malicious, exulting in its own cruelty. Only Goya or Bosch could have made paint render a scene so infernal.

Smoke stung their eyes now and parched their throats

as they breathed the poisoned air. They hardly dared to look behind them again. When they did, they saw a room smothered in smoke and one ravenous, red flame licking the rug on their side of the closed door.

It was better to look the other way. Beyond the fire engines, Tash recognized some of the ushers still in pajamas. The fully clothed were mostly reporters and press photographers. She was surprised to see Bill Brewer among them.

Like everyone else, he was staring up at the house, his face white under the play of red light, his eyeballs glittering whenever they caught the reflection of the flames.

"There's the Governor now!" It was Carlos' voice shouting to firemen. "On that balcony. Bring a ladder. Quick!"

Carlos darted forward until he was on the terrace just below the balcony. He was barefoot, wearing slacks and a shirt, as if he had pulled on the first things that came to hand when the alarm went off.

He looked up and shouted: "Jerry! We couldn't find you anywhere. How the devil did you get up there?"

"Sorry," said Jeremy without offering an explanation.

Tash saw instantly what had happened. When the alarm went off, Carlos and others in the household had failed to find the Governor, because no one would think of looking for him in her rooms at three in the morning.

Now everyone was going to know exactly where he had been, including the reporters and Vivian.

She began to regret her flimsy negligeé and Jerry's tennis shirt with sleeves rolled up and no necktie.

Firemen were dragging a long, heavy ladder up to the balcony with help from Carlos. Its top came to rest against the railing. One fireman held it steady at the bottom and called up the balcony: "Okay, Governor?"

Jeremy stepped back.

"Must I go first?" cried Tash.

He grinned. "What do you think? GOVERNOR RUNS DOWN LADDER LEAVING WOMAN TO FLAMES? A headline like that is all I need now!"

The flagstones looked a long way down. Suddenly, they tilted. To her shame, she knew this was vertigo.

She climbed over the railing and stood for a moment on the narrow ledge beyond it, then turned to face the balcony and Jeremy. His smile encouraged her. One of her feet found the top rung of the ladder behind her where she could not see it. She closed her eyes and began to feel her way down, rung by rung.

She was halfway down when a champagne cork popping sound startled her so she nearly fell. She opened her eyes and caught the last blue-white flare of a press photographer's flash bulb.

She was almost at the bottom when Jeremy called down to Carlos:

"You've got Vivian out?"

"Not yet. The fire seems to have started in her room, and—Jerry! Come back! Don't be a fool!"

Tash looked up just in time to see Jeremy turn away from the balcony and go back into the burning room.

"Tash! Quick!" Carlos lifted her the rest of the way down and ran up the ladder.

The fireman holding the ladder shook his head.

"Are those guys nuts?"

But he followed Carlos up the ladder.

Tash felt an arm around her shoulders. It was Hilary.

She was wearing a mink coat over pajamas, carrying a jewel case, a purse, and a passport. She would always have enough presence of mind to think of her own interests in any crisis.

"He has to do it," said Hilary. "How could he not do it?"

125

"But the firemen are here. They're trained. They've got equipment."

"But they're not married to Vivian. It's been a madhouse. No one in the household knew where anyone was. Even the firemen got lost."

"You're joking!"

"No, it happened. Things like that always happen at moments like this."

Another fireman was going up the ladder, axe in hand. Some of those below turned a hose on the balcony and the open window beyond to clear a path for him.

Hilary's arm tightened around Tash's shoulders. "Stop shaking. It will soon be over."

"Anything I can do?"

Tash turned her head and saw Bill Brewer.

"When it's all over you might take this girl home to her own place," said Hilary. "No one will be able to sleep here the rest of the night."

"Would you like to go now?" Bill asked Tash.

"No." Tash clung to Hilary. She would understand why. Bill might not.

He was looking up at the open window where smoke still boiled onto the balcony. "They've been gone a long time."

"Not really. It only seems long." Hilary looked down at the watch on her wrist. "It's just nine minutes since the alarm went off and just three minutes since Jeremy went back into the house."

"Three minutes is a long time in a fire out of control," said Bill.

Hilary looked at him with exasperation. "Will you kindly be quiet?"

He looked at her in surprise, then caught her glance at Tash and understood.

They heard tires scrape to a gritty stop on gravel. Job

126

came around the corner of the house from the front, fully dressed, running at a jog trot.

He swerved when he saw Tash. "Where's Jerry?"

It was hard to get the words out, but she managed: "He's in the house."

"In the house?" Job shouted. "Why?"

"He went back for Vivian," said Hilary.

"And you let him? Where's Carlos?"

"In the house with Jeremy."

For a moment Job looked as if he were going to hit Hilary. "How could you?"

He turned to the nearest fireman. "You know who I am?"

"Yes, sir, you're Mr. Jackman, the Lieutenant Governor."

"What the hell are you doing out here? It's your job to go in and get the Governor out."

"The Fire Commissioner said—"

"Blast the Fire Commissioner! Take more men and do what I say now."

The fireman started up the ladder, followed by others.

Job was striding through the crowd demanding the Fire Commissioner.

"I had no idea Job Jackman was so devoted to the Governor," said Bill.

"Job managed Jeremy's first campaign," said Hilary. "They've been together ever since. It's symbiosis. Neither can get along without the other. Job is a born campaign manager. As boss of the state machine, he controls party discipline and tactics, but he could never have been elected Lieutenant Governor without Jeremy. He's the one with *mana*, so he commands votes. He will always be out in front, but Job will always be in the background. Warwick, the king-maker many times, but never a king himself."

127

There was a moan from the crowd like the mutter of distant surf. Tash looked up.

Jeremy was standing on the balcony holding something in his arms wrapped in a blanket.

A fireman ran up the ladder and took the burden from him.

"Have you oxygen tanks?" he asked.

"In the ambulance."

Tash was afraid to look at the burden the fireman carried, yet she had to.

Strangely, Vivian might have been asleep. Only the edge of the blanket was singed. Something in her room must have protected her face and hair. The Chinese screen around her bed? Could it have protected her from smoke, too?

"She's still breathing." Jeremy spoke, as if that were the most important thing in the world—and so it was to him at that moment, and therefore, to Tash as well.

He had fared worse than Vivian. His hair and eyebrows were scorched, red burns blotched his face, his hands were already swollen. The white shirt and slacks were grimy with ash. One sleeve was ripped from shoulder to elbow. Every now and then he had to yield to a coughing spell.

Job thrust his way through the crowd to Jeremy.

"You damned fool! You never should have risked—"

Jeremy turned and looked at Job, and Job fell silent.

Carlos was coming down the ladder in no better shape than Jeremy. He was limping because he had burned his bare feet.

Bill proffered cigarettes. In spite of their coughing, Jeremy and Carlos each took one.

After the first, deep drag, Jeremy saw Wilkes and called out to him:

"Is everyone out now?"

128

"Yes, sir." Wilkes came toward them, brushing ash from his sleeves. "The Fire Commissioner says it's under control now. He also says that if the firemen had been five minutes later the whole place would have burned to the ground."

Jeremy grinned the grin the news photographers knew so well. "Then the taxpayers weren't robbed when they spent all that money on a fire alarm years ago?"

"No, but we should have a much more modern alarm now. I can't understand why this one didn't go off when the fire first started."

"Does anyone know how it did start?" asked Tash.

How much Jeremy's grin hid from the world! When it faded as it did now, his face looked older, sadder.

"That's a job for the police as well as the fire department," he said. "Have you any idea now how it started, Wilkes?"

"Not yet, sir. The insurance company will send people here tomorrow. I mean, today. They're the real experts. All we know now is that the fire started in Mrs. Playfair's bedroom."

"How do you know that?"

"It was much fiercer and much farther along there than anywhere else."

"I noticed a porcelain ashtray on her bed," said Carlos. "Perhaps she fell asleep with a burning cigarette in her hand and it fell on the floor. She was still in bed when we found her, as if she had passed from sleep to unconsciousness without waking."

"How could she sleep through the sirens and all the other noise?" demanded Bill. "No one else did."

"She'd had some form of sedative," said Hilary. "Her doctor prescribed two pills every night at bedtime."

"The smoke could have made her unconscious," said

129

Carlos. "That heavy Chinese screen around her bed protected her from flames quite a bit, but the smoke in her room was unbelievable. I almost lost consciousness myself."

Jeremy turned to Wilkes. "What about files and records?"

"All safe. Most of the office wing on the ground floor was spared by the fire, but not by the firemen. They had to cut their way through ground floor walls in order to get at some of the worst spots on the floor above."

"Then none of us can spend the rest of the night here?"

"Oh, no! There are a few spots still smouldering that may burst into flame again. The firemen will be here all night, and I'll mount a guard to prevent looting."

"I'll go back to my own apartment in town," said Tash.

"And the rest of you can come to my place at Fox Run," added Job.

"Thanks," said Jeremy. "But you're pretty far out. I want to be in town near the hospital. Carlos and I can go to a hotel."

"Then I'll drive you and Carlos into town," said Job. "Hilary, I can take you on to Fox Run. Jo Beth will be glad to have you, and Tash—"

"I'm taking Tash home," said Bill.

"Oh?" Jeremy swung around to look at Bill. "You're an old friend of hers, of course. I forgot."

He came over to Tash and took both her hands in his. "Good night, Tash. I'm sorry I got you into all this. I'll call you tomorrow. Take care of her, Bill."

"Don't worry. I will."

Jeremy and Hilary, Job and Carlos all moved away toward the front drive. Bill and Tash followed more slowly.

130

"Why do I have to be taken care of?" mused Tash. "I'm not five years old."

"But you do look nearer fifteen than twenty-five," returned Bill. "Don't worry. Youth is a disease that time cures fast enough."

The telephone wakened her next morning at seven.

"Is that Miss Tatiana Perkins? I have a person-to-person call from Rome. . . ."

"Oh, Daddy, you shouldn't have bothered!"

"What do you expect me to do when my only daughter is all over the front pages of every newspaper? Are you all right?"

"Of course, I am."

She was awake and expecting the second call when it came at eight.

"Miss Tatiana Perkins? Person-to-person call from Boston. . . ."

"Tash, darling, I've just seen the papers!"

"I'm all right, Mother, honestly!"

"But a fire! Would you like me to come down there?"

"No, Mother dear, thanks, but really, the fire is over and I was not hurt . . . Yes, of course, I'm going to rest today."

This time when Tash put down the telephone, she went back to sleep.

The third call woke her at noon.

"May I come to breakfast?" It was Hilary's voice.

"I'd love to see you, but there isn't a scrap of food in the place. The refrigerator is even turned off."

"I'll bring food. You turn on the refrigerator."

Hilary brought oranges and eggs, croissants and fresh butter, coffee, sugar, and cream.

She also brought newspapers.

All the locals, the Washington papers, and even the

New York Times carried a photograph on the front page of Tash coming down the fire ladder in that photogenic, white negligée with Jeremy standing just above her on the balcony.

The news stories were all pretty much alike.

When firemen reached the scene of the fire they had some difficulty finding the Governor himself, who was with a member of his staff, Miss Tatiana Perkins. She was evacuated from her rooms by means of a ladder to one of her windows. The Governor went back into the burning building to bring out his wife, Vivian, with the help of one of his aides, Carlos de Miranda. Mrs. Playfair was taken to the hospital in a serious condition, and she is still on the critical list.

The only other casualty was her maid, Juana Fernandez, whose body was found by firemen early this morning on a flagstone terrace. Apparently, she had fallen from an upstairs window while trying to escape the fire.

"Poor Juana!"

"I know," said Hilary. "Come and have your breakfast."

When Hilary got to her first cigarette, Tash took her second cup of coffee over to the window seat.

"Thanks, Hilary. I needed that breakfast. When I went to stay at Leafy Way I didn't leave anything in the kitchen, not even a can of soup."

"I'll have to go in a little while," said Hilary. "By the way, Bill Brewer thinks you should take this day off."

"Oh, dear!"

"What's the matter?"

"There's something I forgot to tell Bill last night. I'm

132

going to keep my job with Jeremy after all."

Hilary put out her cigarette slowly and carefully. "There may not be a job with Jeremy any more."

"What do you mean?"

"The fire didn't do him any good. The medical verdict is that he must take at least a month's vacation right away. Job, as Lieutenant Governor, will take care of routine state business. Lucky the strike's settled, isn't it? Job could never have handled that on his own."

"And the campaign?"

"Jeremy may not run. It's not just his burns. It's shock. He's been through an ordeal. He can't bounce back in twenty-four hours."

"I understand that, but why should it affect his candidacy? The election isn't until Fall."

"His mood has changed. He may not care about being governor anymore. He may not come back here for years."

"Where is he going?"

"He's gone already. Carlos took him off to Sotavento in the Caribbean. Carlos' mother has a place there. I saw them off at the airport this morning. Jeremy asked me to say good-bye to you for him. He wasn't able to call you after all. He was sorry about that."

"Is Vivian going?"

"No. I've been trying to think of the best way to tell you about that."

"About what?"

"Vivian. She died in the hospital three hours ago. Don't cry! Tash, please . . ."

It was early evening when the doorbell rang again.

Tash pressed the button that turned on the voice box connected with the vestibule downstairs.

"Who's there?"

"Me, Miss Perkins. Boy from Grantley's."

Grantley was the best florist in town.

The boy laid a long, white box on the kitchen table. "You'll be wanting to put these in water."

She shut the door after him, untied the ribbon, and lifted the lid off the box.

A sheaf of long-stemmed red roses lay in a nest of maidenhair fern and green tissue paper. They were just beginning to open their petals, and their fruity scent filled the air around her.

She looked for a card, but there wasn't any. So she knew who had sent them. Only one person had any reason to send her roses without a card.

She put the box down when the telephone rang again. She thought it might be Hilary or Bill or even Gordon, but it was a voice she had never heard before. A woman's voice speaking in the slurred speech of the western counties, and trembling with righteous indignation.

"You dirty whore! You murdering devil! Everyone knows that fire was arson. You set it to kill the Governor's wife so you could marry the Governor. For that you will burn in Hell forever. How do you think she felt when the smoke got into her lungs, and—"

Tash put the telephone back in its cradle, breaking the connection.

In the silence she could still hear that voice going on and on and on. It would not be the only one.

PART II

Fox Run

13

GORDON'S INVITATION to dinner came early in August. He had been extremely busy ever since April, and of course, in his position he had to be careful about being seen in public with anyone who was involved in . . . er . . .

"Scandal?"

"Oh, no, no! Politics. Those of us who have important positions in the civil service are supposed to be completely apolitical."

"I'm completely apolitical now."

That was the truth. She had not heard from Jeremy. There had been newspaper photographs of him with Vivian's parents at her funeral in New York, where she had lived with them before her marriage. He had flown back to Sotavento the next day, according to the news stories. A few postcards from Carlos had told her from time to time that Jeremy was "getting better," but there was nothing about his return. Tash was beginning to wonder if he would ever want to come back.

She accepted Gordon's invitation in the selfish hope that other evenings with other men might lay Jeremy's ghost eventually. She had forgotten how powerfully contrast can evoke opposites.

Gordon fussed over a choice of restaurant, sent his fish

back to the kitchen because he claimed it was frozen, not fresh, and found something wrong with the wine as well. By the time he had thus paraded his connoisseurship twice, their table was the most conspicuous in the room.

"Dessert?"

"No, thank you."

"Well, I want dessert. *Garçon!* Waiter!"

Two minutes later Gordon was haranguing the waiter for bringing him a soggy *millefeuilles* pastry.

Now he had taken out his temper three times on the hapless waiters, he became mellow over coffee and Benedictine.

"I'm glad you're back on the newspaper."

"Are you?"

Something in her voice made him look up. "Aren't you glad?"

"Not particularly. I liked being at Leafy Way."

"Oh, I suppose there were perquisites. Tennis courts and all that. You practically lived there, didn't you?"

"That was part of the job."

"A silly way to do things. I know that whenever I tried to get you on the telephone there I had an awful time. They kept saying you were out or busy or something."

"I usually was."

"Well, I quite missed our little evenings together. You're so refreshing after the sophisticated, glamourous women I see in Washington all the time."

"Thanks!"

"You know I never did like him."

"Who?"

"Jeremy Playfair. Too young for his job. And too flashy. Nothing solid about him. He'd never get anywhere in the civil service."

"You didn't know him, did you?"

"Well, I never actually met him, but, of course, in my

138

position I do hear a great deal of gossip in Washington, and the things I've heard about him—"

"Gordon!"

"What's the matter?"

"Either you take me home now or I'm going alone. I am not going to sit here and listen to Washington tattle about the Governor. I got to know him well when I was on his staff, and I do like him."

Gordon stared at her, mouth ajar. "I never thought you'd feel any loyalty to him."

"Well, now you know. I do."

Gordon signaled the waiter for the check. "This is rather awkward."

"Why?"

"Because now I suppose I can't say something I had planned to say to you."

"Why not?"

"You won't like it."

"Then isn't it better left unsaid?"

"No, I think it is my duty, Tash, to warn you against Jeremy Playfair. He is not a suitable companion for a girl of your type and—"

Tash rose. "I doubt if you have the slightest idea what type of girl I am, Gordon. Indeed, there are times when I like to think I am not a type at all, but an individual. Please just stop talking about Jerry."

"Jerry? Is that what you call him?"

"Yes. Why not?"

Gordon said no more on the subject. When he took her home he looked at her forgivingly when she did not ask him in for a nightcap, and said: "Tash, no matter what happens, no matter how deeply you may become involved in a rather unseemly situation, I do want you to know that, if you need me, you may always count on my friendship."

139

As she was unlocking the door to her apartment, she heard her telephone ringing. Leaving the key in the lock, she ran into a long slide like a baseball player to grab the telephone before it stopped ringing.

For one wild moment she had hoped she might hear an operator's voice saying: *Person-to-person call from Sotavento,* but it was only Bill Brewer.

"I've been ringing you all evening."

"I was out at dinner."

"So I deduced. The insurance company has completed its investigation of Leafy Way. I am going out there tomorrow to get a final story on the causes of the fire. Want to come? You were a witness. You might think of questions to ask them that would not occur to me."

"Wild horses wouldn't keep me away!"

"Then I'll pick you up at ten o'clock."

Tash was waiting for him downstairs when he arrived. As she slid into the passenger seat beside him, she said: "Why has this investigation taken so long? This is August. The fire was in April."

"It was unusually thorough. They must be sure of their facts in this case. If the fire was the work of a torch—"

"A torch?"

"Police jargon for an arsonist. If this was arson, it may have been an attempt to assassinate the Governor."

"His wife was the one who died."

"But the fire could have been meant for him. Her death could have been incidental."

For the first time Tash wondered if Jeremy had escaped death because he had been in her rooms when the fire started, something no arsonist could possibly have foreseen. In Vivian's bedroom or in his own adjoining bedroom, he might have had as little chance as Vivian herself. It was in her room that the fire started and blazed most fiercely.

"But who would want to kill Jeremy?"

"There were some pretty violent people involved in that strike. Remember? Two men were killed and several injured."

"But Jeremy settled the strike!"

"And by so doing made the Barloventan political exiles his implacable enemies. They say he betrayed them by breaking all sorts of promises he made to them in the beginning."

"I don't believe that. Do you?"

"Probably just a misunderstanding. Verbal agreements are tricky things. But whether it's true or not, they believe it and they are fanatics, so that gives them a motive for killing him."

Tash fell silent as the car turned into the familiar Leafy Way drive.

The façade in front was not so bad. Just some windows boarded up where glass had been broken. It was only when Bill and she walked around the house to where she could see her own windows and Vivian's, that she caught her breath.

The mild August sunshine fell gently on a charred and lunatic chaos. Great holes gaped in once solid walls of brick and lathe and plaster. Insulation leaked from between inner and outer walls in the form of powdered ash.

A lilac silk quilt, grimy with cinders, dangled from an upstairs window. A portable television set lay on one side just inside an open door. Its plastic case had been melted by intense heat into a fantastic, free-form shape that had no rational relation to the shape of circuits and wiring inside the case.

They walked into a drawing room and saw a bucket of dirty water standing on top of a mahogany piano. Some paintings in oil stacked in a fireplace looked as if the paint had become soft and sticky. Underfoot, shards of broken glass and splintered wood and a dozen varieties of ash were all melded by rain and dew into a thick, gritty mush.

"They haven't even begun to clean up!" cried Tash.

"They can't," said Bill. "There's an unusually large amount of insurance money at stake. There were absolute orders from the insurance company that nothing must be moved or even touched until their investigation was completed. They've been out here for weeks, photographing, sifting, and analyzing in the most minute detail. The Police Commissioner and the Fire Commissioner backed the insurance company, because they're even more anxious to know whether this was arson or not."

Tash looked up at exposed beams overhead that were badly charred. "Will they have to be replaced?"

"Probably, and that alone is about the most expensive thing you can do to a house."

"Couldn't those charred beams be encased in wood paneling?"

"They could, but if you did that you'd get a horrid smell of burnt wood on every rainy day."

At last they came to the Florida Room. The wicker and rattan furniture had vanished in the flames. All that remained were the iron and glass tables, the stone floor, the marble chimney piece.

It was there that Captain Wilkes met them.

"We've seen enough of the downstairs," said Bill. "Is it possible to go upstairs where the fire started?"

"You mean poor Mrs. Playfair's room? Yes, it's safe to go up there now. We've braced the stairway and shored up the floor in several places. We had to do that before we could go up ourselves."

Wilkes led them to the door of Vivian's room.

The taffeta curtains were gone. The paneling that had

not been repainted since the eighteenth century was blistered and black. The whole room was black, brown, yellow, and gray now. Even the bed had burned after Jeremy and Carlos got Vivian out. The linen sheets were scorched rags. The screen of black lacquer and mother-of-pearl, that was supposed to have protected Vivian when the fire first began, was now itself a mass of cinders and ashes turning to powdery dust beneath their feet.

Something glinted there. Tash kicked the dust aside with the toe of her shoe and discovered two dimes.

"Did one of you drop these?"

Both men shook their heads.

"Better keep them," said Wilkes. "Found money is supposed to be lucky."

Bill touched one of the curtains. It crumbled into flakes. He looked at Wilkes. "Well? What do you think? Was it arson? That's what I came here today to find out. What do the insurance people say?"

"They say not. In spite of all the money involved, they have to say that because they have not turned up any evidence of arson."

"Do you agree?"

"I have doubts, but no evidence, so I can't arrest anybody."

"Do you suspect any person or group of persons?"

"Not even that. It's just a feeling I have, an insight, a Gestalt thing."

"How do the insurance people account for the fire?"

"Mrs. Playfair had the habit of sleeping in bed. That's her ashtray still there on the bed now." He pointed to a few shards of broken china, white with touches of gilt and pale blue and green that had once been a forget-me-not pattern. "Some of the ashes on the counterpane were analyzed. They proved to be cigarette paper and tobacco."

143

"In other words, she took her sleeping pills and dozed off with a lighted cigarette in one hand?" said Bill.

"Or in her ashtray where it could have rolled off onto the bed when she turned over in her sleep," answered Wilkes. "Sometimes the smoker wakes in time, but not if he's drunk, or taking sedatives as Mrs. Playfair was."

"I don't believe it!" said Tash. "I saw Vivian Playfair in this room a few hours before the fire. She was smoking then and it worried me. I made her promise she wouldn't smoke in bed anymore. I think she meant to keep that promise."

"Perhaps she meant to," said Wilkes. "But she was subject to loss of memory. She may have forgotten."

"Wouldn't an arsonist need something more than a cigarette?" asked Bill. "Lighter fluid or kerosene?"

"Hardly necessary," said Wilkes. "Cigarettes have started thousands of fires. Most of them have a chemical added to keep them burning when the smoker isn't inhaling. If you've ever rolled your own without any chemical additive, you'll remember how easily they go out."

"Then what is bothering you if it isn't the cigarette?" demanded Bill. "And don't fob me off with vague stuff about Gestalt insight."

"All right, I'll tell if you won't print it. Scout's honor?"

"Scout's honor."

"Why the hell didn't that fire alarm go off sooner? It was heard first at three A.M. Our chemists think that the fire in this room had been burning then for at least a half an hour. It's not the most modern fire alarm system in the world but it's adequate, and we did check it once a week. We checked it three days before the fire, and it was in good working order then. It's detectors don't wait for flames. They are sensitive to heat and smoke. There was a lot of heat and smoke here before three o'clock. Why didn't the alarm go off?"

144

"Have you checked the detectors since the fire?"

"They're too badly burned for us to check them now. Arson has a way of destroying most of the evidence that it ever occurred. So what it all boils down to is a verdict of not proven."

"What it all boils down to is no story I can print." Bill sighed. "I'm used to that. When I retire I'm going to write a book called *The Unprinted History of the Twentieth Century.*"

"A better title would be *The Unprintable History of the Twentieth Century,*" said Tash.

"I'll tell you what you can print," said Wilkes. "An editorial article saying that Leafy Way must have the most modern and efficient fire alarm system in the world before any governor lives here again."

When they were in the car once more on their way back to town, Bill said, "Tash, there's something I've been meaning to say to you for some time. I know you liked Jeremy Playfair, but people who are not used to heights can get dizzy up there where the air is pretty rarefied. I'm glad you're out of it now. You are out of it, aren't you?"

Tash laughed aloud. "You, too?"

"Who else has broached the subject?"

"Gordon Freese. Did you really think I would stop seeing Jeremy now after all he's been through? He probably won't need me anymore when he comes back, but if he does, I'm not going to ignore him."

"If he comes back," said Bill. "There is a persistent rumor that he will resign now. After all, Job Jackman is doing a pretty good job as a governor pro tem."

Tash was the first out of the car. Bill followed her into her vestibule. She looking into her mailbox.

"There's a letter. No, it's a cable. I've been out so much they couldn't reach me by telephone."

She took it in at one glance, and then handed it to Bill.

145

GOVERNOR RETURNING FRIDAY RESUMING RE-ELECTION
CAMPAIGN STOP CAN YOU TAKE SAME JOB STOP WOULD BE
APPRECIATED REGARDS CARLOS

Reply prepaid: Carlos de Miranda, Cayo Siesta, Sotavento.

"How will you answer this?" asked Bill.
"In just two words: DELIGHTED TASH."

Next morning Hilary telephoned.

"I've persuaded Job to turn over his place, Fox Run, to Jeremy until Leafy Way can be occupied again. Job and Jo Beth are moving to a hotel in town. I thought it might be a good idea to go out to Fox Run today and see what needs to be done before Jeremy gets here, but I have a problem. My car's is in the garage for a check up. Could you drive me in your car? . . . I'll be ready and waiting for you in half an hour."

In spite of the sultry August day, Hilary looked as cool and neat as usual in ice-green linen with dark green shoes and smoothly immaculate hair. Tash herself could never attain that each-hair-in-its-place grooming. Just looking at Hilary made her feel blowzy.

Hilary told her to take an interstate highway and go toward the eastern part of the state where there was seacoast and sandy beaches.

The end-of-summer feeling was everywhere in the dusty leaves, the breathless heat, the late-blooming goldenrod and asters and loosestrife edging ditches along the road. Most of all it was in a single branch of sumac that had already turned bright scarlet, looking weirdly unnatural in a world where everything else was green.

"Why Fox Run?" asked Tash.

"This used to be fox-hunting country. Have you ever read Bayard Taylor's novel *The Story of Kennett*? It's about fox hunting in Kennett Square long ago, and that's

146

just across the border in Pennsylvania. Job says his house is surrounded by a little wilderness, where foxes often went to earth. Fox Run is actually the name of a road."

They left the highway for a rougher road winding through the woods. Suddenly, they came out into the sunlight, where trees had been cut away on both sides of the road. On their left a private road led through meadows and paddocks to a tall angular Victorian house, standing in a sweep of lawn about half a mile away. A few shade trees clustered around the lawn. Beyond, stood a stone barn bigger than the house itself.

"Fox Run used to be a working farm," said Hilary.

Tash followed the road to a front door under a porte-cochère. Hilary got out looking around as critically as if she were going to take a long lease on the house for herself.

"It's not Leafy Way," she sighed. "But I suppose it will do. Jo Beth says the barn is a guest house now. We can put executive offices there."

Hilary rang the bell.

The door was opened by the chief usher from Leafy Way. He smiled broadly when he saw them.

"Settling down all right?" asked Hilary.

"Everything unpacked and under control, ma'am. Shall I show you round?"

"Please do."

The furniture was Job's, good, solid reproductions of old pieces that would have passed for originals if they had been a little shabbier. The only Playfair things were linen, table silver, and a few books and pictures, all rescued from Leafy Way. Tash was pleased to see *Dragon Playing with a Pearl* among the pictures.

"Let's see the garden," said Hilary.

The usher opened a glass door and they stepped outside.

"No terrace," muttered Hilary.

"But a beautiful lawn," said Tash. "And comfortable garden furniture."

The open space was surrounded by the woods as by a wall, but looking west, you could see hills far in the distance above the treetops. Today there was a heat haze and the hills looked insubstantial as folds of soft, gray chiffon against the hot, blue sky.

"I like this place," said Tash. "I could be happy here."

As they strolled back toward the house, Tash saw a flash of movement through an open French window on the ground floor.

"Tash! Hilary!" Carlos stepped through the window with a brilliant smile. His teeth were stark white against the deep tan he had acquired in Sotavento.

"What a surprise to find you both here!" He clasped Tash's hand in his right and Hilary's in his left. "We're only just off the plane."

"We?" said Hilary.

"Yes." Carlos raised his voice. "Jerry, I've got a surprise for you. A nice surprise!"

"But you said you were coming back Friday."

"This morning we found we could get a plane today, so we took it."

Jeremy came out of the house, smiling, too, but not quite as broadly as Carlos. His fair skin had tanned pinkish rather than brown. He looked thinner. He seemed quieter.

"It's good to find you both here," he said. "I didn't expect a welcome like this."

"We just came to look the place over today," said Hilary. "We could probably move in tomorrow. At least, Tash and the secretariat could. I don't have a job any more."

"Oh, yes, you do, if you want one. I've never had a social secretary, but I am going to need someone for that job now."

148

"Are you still going to open your campaign out west?" They were the first words Tash had spoken since Jeremy appeared.

"Yes," he answered pleasantly, but impersonally. "Job is convinced it will help with the western vote."

The chief usher was coming over the grass, his smile even broader now that Jeremy and Carlos were here. Would they like to have dinner served here tonight?

"Dinner?" repeated Jeremy. "Nothing so elaborate. Just a buffet supper out here *al fresco*. I suppose there is food in the house?"

"Oh, yes, sir. Mrs. Jackman saw to that. What time would you like supper?"

"In about an hour, and bring us some mint juleps now."

As the sun was setting, they ate cold poached salmon with green mayonnaise. It seemed to Tash that Jeremy had changed in many ways. He didn't talk so much. He didn't smile so often. When he wasn't smiling, he looked older than she had ever seen him.

When Hilary was talking to him, Tash took the opportunity to speak to Carlos in a low voice. "Is he all right?"

"Much better than he was," answered Carlos in a voice as low. "For a long time he didn't read newspapers or write letters or do anything but swim and sleep."

"I wondered why he didn't write."

"He was like a man in a trance. For weeks. The physical scars of the fire healed quickly enough, but there were times when I thought the psychic scar of Vivian's death would never heal at all. He felt himself responsible for everything that had happened to her."

"How could he?"

"That's the way we all feel when someone we love dies. You're too young to know about that. Fortunately, it passes, like everything else. I knew it had passed for Jeremy when he began looking at newspaper headlines

149

again. That was when I first urged him to come back to all the problems he has here. I think that's what he needs now."

Hilary was not lowering her voice. "Oh, this is a nice enough place in its way, but there's no swimming pool."

Jeremy laughed for the first time.

"You haven't looked at a map. If you had, you'd know that we don't need a swimming pool here. We're within a mile of the sea. Job has his own ocean beach, and that's something I've always envied him."

"What about pollution?"

"I don't think it's got this far yet. Even if it has, I'd rather have a polluted sea than a chlorinated pool. When I got your letter about Fox Run, Hilary, my first thought was the beach."

"Oh, I forgot, I've got some mail for you at home," said Hilary. "Job has been handling all state business, but he turned the personal stuff over to me. I only forwarded the ones that were really important, but you ought to see the others now."

"Fan letters?"

"Lots."

"I'd like to see a sampling of those. They are a useful barometer when an election's pending."

"Then I'd better be getting home, so I can sort them out tonight and bring all the personal files over here the first thing tomorrow morning. Tash, we came in your car, so if you're ready now . . . ?"

Carlos intervened. "I'm going back to town myself this evening, so I can drive you, Hilary, if Tash would like to stay a little longer."

It was done smoothly without a ripple on the surface, but the net result was to leave Tash alone with Jeremy, and she could not help realizing that Carlos was aware of this.

She stood with Jeremy under the porte-cochère while Carlos and Hilary drove away.

"I'd like to show you that beach now," said Jeremy. "Do you have time?"

"Oh, yes, all the time in the world."

"I'll have to borrow your car. Carlos drove off with mine."

It was strange to be a passenger in her own car with Jeremy driving, and yet it was pleasant.

They drove through the woods for only a few minutes before she heard the mutter of surf.

"I had no idea we were so near the sea!"

"A little uncanny, isn't it? Woods always make you feel that you're inland. This road is called Further Lane, and that's uncanny, too. Farther is the word you use for distance in space, but further really means distance in time. I'm always expecting to drive into the eighteenth century on this road."

The car shot out of the trees. Now there were sand dunes on either side, with wild grass streaming in the wind from their crests like long hair.

The road ended in a turnaround at the top of a steep rise in its gradient, probably to accommodate one of the dunes.

There was no one else there at this hour of the night. Jeremy halted the car at the very edge of the macadam and switched off the headlights.

There was only starlight now. All they could see of the ocean was the foamy, white edge of waves creaming on the sand. Beyond, there was only a black void, without any sign of an horizon, that seemed to go on forever. Without surf, there would have been no sea; without stars, no sky.

Jeremy switched off the engine and began to speak in the sudden stillness. "Tash, there are some things you

151

ought to know now. I loved Vivian, but she did not love me. She knew a divorce would hurt my future, and she cared enough about me not to want that. So she hesitated, feeling trapped, bored and unhappy. A generation ago she might have taken to drink. In this generation, she took to drugs.

"For a long time I knew she was unhappy, but I didn't know why. I suppose she was trying to spare me as long as she could. I didn't even think of divorce. How could I when she was so obviously in some kind of trouble?"

"Why are you telling me all this?"

"Because I don't want you to feel guilty. You must not get the idea that you came between Vivian and me. That would be too heavy a burden of guilt for anyone like you.

"Vivian and I had been divorced emotionally before you and I ever met. She and I were trapped. Sooner or later, one of us was bound to fall in love with someone else. It was chance or Fate that I was the one, and that I fell in love with you.

"Nothing you said or did made me do it. I just did. And now, I must know if you fell in love with me. I've never been sure. Did you?"

He waited for an answer in words, but the only answer she could give him was in her eyes.

Swiftly he bowed his head to kiss her lips. She had never known a kiss like that before. Her arms lifted to draw him closer to her heart, and everything else was forgotten in mutual surrender.

PART III

Desolation Bend

14

EVERYONE AT FOX RUN knew they were lovers, and that they would marry after a decent interval, but no one in the household ever showed the slightest awareness of this. The lovers were cosseted in a snug cocoon of discreet silence. The only exceptions were occasional glances in their direction tinged with envy. There are few people, however cynical, who do not hanker a little after the rare experience of happiness in love which passes so many by. This envy was wistful, quite without jealousy or malice.

The conspiracy of forebearance included the press. No hint of the truth appeared in any newspaper. Even the most intrusive gossip columnists left this story alone. After all, Tash had no enemies in public life, and Jeremy, who did, had won the sympathy of most people by his ordeal on the night of the fire. Everyone who knew them seemed glad that the Governor had found a way to mend his broken life.

But what about the invisible multitude out there beyond the newspapers and television screens? What was being said by people who didn't know them?

There was one clue: the letters addressed to Jeremy or Tash that came pouring into the mailing department of

the secretariat at Fox Run, some signed, some anonymous, and about thirty-five percent abusive. The largest
number of these came from the western counties, where
Jeremy was going to open his re-election campaign in the
next few days.

The minds behind these letters were as inflexible as
muscles in spasm and locked onto a few archetypal ideas
with the tenacity of rigor mortis. Once they got hold of
an idea they seemed almost physically incapable of letting it go, the way a steel needle is physically incapable
of separating itself from a magnet.

They were now denouncing Jeremy as "soft on com-
munism" because his strike settlement had led to
renewed trade with Barlovento, which had a government they considered leftist. Egged on by Barloventan
political exiles, they wanted to believe anything nasty
they heard about the "traitor" as they called him. So they
seized upon rumors of the role Tash played in his life
with gleeful avidity.

She was not just the Whore of Babylon. She was Lady
MacBeth. One letter even quoted: *Infirm of purpose! Give
me the daggers. . . .*

Job was the one who first showed Tash a sampling of
the letters. He did it one afternoon in her own office in
the stone barn. He gave her a little time to recover while
he clipped and lighted a fresh cigar.

"Does Jerry know you're showing me these?"

"No, I'd like to keep this between you and me."

"What do you want me to do?"

"Would you be willing to give up Jeremy and not
marry him?"

"You can't be serious."

"I was never more serious in my life. These letters
don't just accuse you of carrying on with Jeremy before
Vivian died. They accuse you of murdering her. They all

imply that you set the fire at Leafy Way, so that she would be killed and you could then marry Jeremy without his having to go through the politically damaging process of a contested divorce."

"Job, you know that's all absurd."

"I know it, but the people who write these letters don't, and that's what counts. If you marry Jeremy now, you are giving yourself the motive for murder they have already assigned to you."

"There's no evidence the fire was arson."

"That's what the insurance company says now, but Wilkes is still working on it. If he turns up something, and you are the only person with a motive for killing Vivian, the police are going to question you very closely indeed. Headlines, television commentators, gossip columnists, the works. Why marry him? Aren't you happy enough as you are now?"

Tash managed to keep her temper and said quietly: "We want to have children."

"Forget it! At least, for the time being. In three or four years the whole thing may die down. Or somebody else may be accused of the murder. I'm only advising you this way for your own good."

Tash laughed. "Am I supposed to thank you?"

"You don't have to, but I hope you won't tell Jeremy how I feel about this."

"Of course I shall tell Jeremy. We don't have secrets from each other."

She did not tell him all the details of her conversation with Job for fear it would make him angry with Job. She merely said that Job wanted them to postpone their marriage until the spate of scurrilous letters had died down.

Jeremy took this lightly. "Poor old Job! Always seeing lost elections under the bed. People who write letters like that are crackpots, like those people who still think the earth is flat. According to the last Gallup Poll, I've got a majority of voters in my camp already. I think we should be married as soon as the election is over. It was you who thought we should wait a year, but if Job or anyone else thinks I'm going to wait four or five years . . . Tash, you're not listening!"

"There's so much malice in these letters," she answered. "It's beginning to frighten me."

Aside from this Tash was happy as she had never been happy before in her whole life. Working with Jeremy on the western speeches was not work now; it was play. Never before had she walked with such a light foot and a high heart. Never before had the scent of roses been so sweet or the sound of music so joyous or the sunshine so bright.

Like most happy people she wanted others to be as happy as herself, and this made her more tolerant than she had ever been before. The sharp eye for other people's failings which had once spiced her newspaper column was gone. Even poor Gordon Freese was invited to dinner at Fox Run one evening because she thought it would gratify him, as it obviously did.

The Victorians had preached: Be good and you will be happy; but there is something in the opposite idea: Be happy and you will be good.

Hilary was characteristically concerned about the clothes she and Tash would wear on the western trip.

"Won't our ordinary clothes do?"

"Yours won't, dear. You haven't appeared in a single new thing since I first met you."

"What should I get?"

"It will be suit weather out there at this time of year. You should get at least one new suit, very plain and very chic. Those rich western women will look like *singes endimanchés.*"

158

"Overdressed? I should have thought the opposite."

"It's an over-reaction to the Davy Crockett notions of the males out there. You must show them how eastern women combine severity with elegance."

"Won't they mistake what you call severity for dowdiness if they're not used to it?"

"No. They may be hillbillies, but they're still women. They'll know chic when they see it, whether they know how to achieve it themselves or not. Get some good shoes and a small hat so they can see your face."

"Why any hat at all?"

"You'll be in an open car most of the time. You'll need something to keep your hair in order. There will be a lot of formal occasions and hats are a part of formality."

"You do seem to have worked everything out to the minutest detail."

"It's important. You're not just a member of the staff anymore. They've all heard of you, and they probably all know you're going to marry the Governor. The younger and smarter you look, the less likely they are to think of you as Lady MacBeth. A great deal is forgiven to the young and reasonably pretty, so put your best foot forward."

Somewhat reluctantly, Tash drew most of her savings out of the bank and went to the shop that Hilary called a boutique. The prices alarmed her, but she had to live up to Jeremy now, so she gritted her teeth and chose two suits, one light, one dark, with blouses and shoes and hats that went with them. She liked the light suit best, a short jacket and skirt of sheer wool in a subtle robin's egg blue. The brown velvet collar made her eyes still more brown. The small hat, shaped like a crown, was brown velvet, too.

"That's the one to wear on special occasions," said Hilary. "And, for God's sake, no jewels and no furs."

159

"You wear mink all the time."

"That's different. I'm an old woman, and it's the only warm winter coat I've got. I can't afford a new one of the same quality in any other material."

Carlos was the advance man for the trip, sent ahead of the Governor and his party by ten days so he could organize Jeremy's reception by town and county officers and local district leaders. A tight schedule had to be set up so that all kinds of political clubs and civic associations would be given an opportunity to welcome the Governor.

After five days, Carlos sent back a tentative itinerary for the Governor's approval.

They were to fly to the one jet port in the western counties, arriving August 9th, and then proceed in a fleet of cars with many stops along the way that would take them altogether until September 8th.

"Carlos will have to change those dates," said Job. "I'm meeting the Chairman of the National Committee in Washington on August ninth, hoping to get the President to speak at one of your meetings once the campaign really gets going in the east. I can't and won't postpone anything as important as that."

"Why don't you meet us afterward then?" said Jeremy. "You could fly out west alone and get there August tenth or eleventh."

The program included luncheons and dinners in small cities and large towns, nights spent in private houses or country inns, and what Job called "whistle stops"—brief halts for ten-minute speeches in village halls or schools along the way from one town to another.

Carlos described one of these whistle stops in a letter to Jeremy.

"Not even a hamlet. Just a crossroads, with one building. When we get there, you'll wonder why we're stop-

160

ping at all, so I'd better explain. It's partly because that crossroads is the social center for about thirty big sheep ranchers who've been rooting for you all over the county, but it's also because this is one of the most beautiful places I've ever seen in my life, and I want you and Tash to see it, too.

"You know how most rivers flow in valleys, so when you get a river view, you can't get a close-up of mountain tops at the same time? Here, by some freak of nature, you have both. The river is right up there among the peaks of high mountains. You can hardly believe it even when you see it: five peaks soaring to the sky, cliffs plunging down a thousand feet or so to valleys below, and there, at the top, where it has no business to be, a river.

"That view is so improbable, it's unreal. You get an eerie feeling just looking at it. At the same time, you have a feeling of awe, as if the whole planet was unfolded and laid out at your feet. What people call an 'airplane view.' Didn't Anatole France say, 'My front door opens on the infinite'? That's exactly the way you'd feel if you had a house in a place like that."

"These romantic Latins!" said Jeremy to Hilary. "Carlos has made that day's schedule much too tight just to get this weird place in. You'll have to cross it off the itinerary. If you don't, we might be late for our last big meeting, the one at the new jet port in Boone City before we take off for home. That's more important than any whistle stop, however picturesque."

Hilary drew a blue pencil through the "weird place."

"Carlos has done pretty well," she said. "This is the only stop you've had to cross off his itinerary."

When Tash and Jeremy were alone together they spent some time discussing their first meetings, as lovers are apt to do.

"From the first time we met we wanted each other,"

161

said Jeremy. "Only we didn't know it consciously at all. When Nature is bent on procreation she pushes us all around like pawns in a chess game, and the fascinating thing is that at the conscious level we always have perfectly good reasons for what we are doing that have nothing to do with procreation at all.

"Why did I want you as a speech writer? Why did you accept immediately and give up your column to do so? It was the only way we could have got to know each other so quickly. Why did I kiss you the evening the strike was settled unless it was because I loved you? I only kissed Hilary to have an excuse for kissing you. I realized that at the time, and yet I thought both kisses were sexless.

"What was the real reason you resigned? To break up our relationship? It was the very thing most likely to stimulate our relation, as you must have known unconsciously.

"Why did I come to your rooms late the night of the fire when I could so easily have talked to you the next morning? Because I wanted you and didn't realize it at the conscious level.

"Each of us was in an intolerable situation. I was trying to go on loving a wife who didn't love me. You were telling yourself that you would never fall in love because of what had happened to your parents. Something had to give. If it hadn't been the fire, it would have been something else that brought everything to a head."

"What about people who don't want children? Doesn't Nature push them around?"

"There aren't any. Unconsciously, everybody wants children. That's why we have over-population."

The night before they left for the west, Tash lay awake in his arms long after he had gone to sleep. This time at Fox Run had been so happy for her that she hated to think of leaving the place even for a little while.

He stirred and opened his eyes. "Why are you awake?"

"I don't know."

He took her in his arms.

"It's like dying . . ." she whispered.

And later he told her: "That's what the French call it: *la petite mort*, the little death."

15

THE MOMENT YOU stepped out of the plane you knew you were in high country. Wave after frozen wave of mountains ringed the mesa where the airport stood, brilliant in their autumn livery of scarlet and gold. There was a snap in the air, more like October than August, and it tasted clean as spring water.

Jeremy looked up at a sky, brilliant as a blue flame, and then brought his gaze down to the funereal, black limousine provided for his use.

"Mr. Mayor, it's criminal to drive in a car like that on a day like this. Isn't there an open car I could have?"

Captain Wilkes sprang forward. "Governor, for reasons of security I asked for a closed car and—"

"Stop right there, Wilkes. I came here to see people. In a big city, where crowds are large and anonymous, there's some excuse for holding them at arm's length, but not here in this country, where crowds are small and everybody knows everybody else."

The Mayor beamed. It was one of the most cherished illusions of the region that all city folk were quiet, treacherous, and violent, while all country people were, like country music, loud, honest, and peaceable.

In a rich, west-country accent, the Mayor assured the Governor that they were all home folks here in Boone

164

County, that they had all voted for Jeremy Playfair, that they were all sure tickled to death to have him with them on this beautiful autumn day, the kind of weather they had most of the year here, in God's own country, and the last thing the Governor needed was a closed car. The Mayor's good friend, the President of the Board of Aldermen, would be only too happy to provide the Governor with a convertible, so he could ride with the top down.

Wilkes was not pleased. He insisted on driving the car himself, with Carlos beside him in the front seat and a motorcycle escort deployed around the car.

Jeremy and the Mayor shared the back seat. The Mayor's wife, Hilary, and Tash followed in a second car that was closed.

That afternoon there was a reception at the Mayor's house attended by apparently everyone of the slightest importance in the county. Tash had never seen so many mink shrugs and diamond earrings all at once. Hilary was right, as usual. The only way Tash could compete with these women was by wearing no jewels or furs at all.

"I thought hillbillies were poor," she said to Hilary. "Where does all the money come from?"

"Oil. Whether it's Middle East or Southwest, oil just loves a backwoods community where it can upset all ecological and economic patterns. Did you ever hear of anybody finding an oil well in Manhattan or Paris?"

In the receiving line, the Governor shook more than five thousand hands. Most of them had the good sense to move on quickly, but there were, as always, a few who held up the line in order to tell the Governor that they had once met his great uncle, or that they didn't agree with his last speech about regulating the sale of weed killers.

When this happened, Carlos allowed just one question

165

or comment, and then, as soon as Jeremy had responded, eased the exhibitionist along with a smile so that the line was not clogged for any length of time.

When, at last, the receiving line came to an end, Jeremy tried to cross the room to Tash, but his way was barred by a solid hedge of the loyal and the curious. A governor cannot push his way through a crowd. Fortunately, an A.D.C. can. Indeed that's what he's for. Carlos was there immediately, facing Jeremy but walking backward, glancing over his shoulder to avoid collision, and so clearing a path where Jeremy could move without either hindrance or embarrassment.

Tash heard a girl in the crowd say: "I am never going to wash that hand again!"

This she reported to Hilary. "Do they think an elected politician has the King's Touch?"

"Probably." Hilary frowned. "I don't like this atavistic *Golden Bough* stuff. We all know what happens to sacred kings in the end."

Job flew in by commercial jet the next day, just in time for a chamber of commerce luncheon at the county seat.

Tash was the first to spot him, standing alone in a doorway of the big hotel ballroom, for once hesitant and almost shy. As soon as others recognized him, he got a rousing welcome and became the hero of the occasion.

To Tash, the incident seemed a little contrived. Had the Washington trip really been necessary? Or was the whole thing a device for making a dramatic entrance?

During the next weeks they were lavishly entertained in private houses by hospitable strangers. The pace was so demanding that it was a relief to spend their last night out west at a mountain inn, where there were no other guests by arrangement, and they no longer felt they were on parade.

Jeremy and Tash ordered breakfast on a stone terrace

166

with a view of the whole mountain range.

When the waiter left them alone together, he kissed her quickly. "I love you, Tash."

"Someone might come along."

"Who cares?" He was kissing her less quickly when Carlos walked out on the terrace with a newspaper clipping in one hand.

Jeremy waved it away. "Not before breakfast!"

"I'm sorry, but I think you should see this now."

"For or against us?"

"Against. It's in the local rag this morning and it's a honey! Real, old-fashioned, frontier journalism."

Jeremy began to read while Tash looked over his shoulder.

It was an editorial article headed:

OUR WHIZ KID GOVERNOR

This morning we have in our midst a brash, young governor who represents all that is effete and decadent in the devious Eastern Establishment of this state.

We opposed him during the last election when he captured his high office by using questionable electioneering practices. Nothing he has done since has changed our view of him. Jeremy Playfair is immature, irresponsible, frivolous, and totally unfit for any public office higher than that of assistant dogcatcher.

His reckless attempt to meddle in foreign affairs by breaking the dock strike and resuming trade relations with the treacherous Reds in Barlovento may plunge the whole country into a Caribbean war at any moment.

The bill he has just signed abolishing capital pun-

167

ishment leaves honest citizens with no defense against skyrocketing crime.

We must find a way to get rid of this arrogant young man before he has time to do any more harm to our beloved state and our great country.

Turn the rascal out!

NOW!

"Quite a mess of words!" Jeremy grinned. "Brash, effete, devious, decadent, questionable, immature, irresponsible, frivolous, unfit, reckless, arrogant. Have I left any out?"

"Don't just laugh, Jerry!" The faint trace of Spanish accent became more marked when Carlos was upset. "This is serious."

"How can you expect me to take a thing like that seriously? That's not an editorial. That's just graffiti. They'll be scrawling on the walls next: *Jeremy Playfair, go home!*"

"I can't believe it," said Tash. "All the people we've met have been so nice to us."

"You haven't met the people who write such editorials," said Carlos. "Or the people who read such editorials."

"I still can't take it seriously," said Jeremy. "I've had worse things said about me a thousand times."

"No, you haven't," retorted Carlos. That they should call you bad names like 'decadent' is nothing. I agree. But that line at the end: *We must find a way to get rid of this arrogant young man. . . .* It reminds me of another line: *Will no one rid me of this troublesome priest?* Wilkes doesn't like it either. He wants you to go in a closed car today."

"Oh, Jerry, please do!" said Tash.

"Afraid they'll start throwing rotten eggs at me? I've

always used open cars in my campaigns, and I'm not going to stop now because of one crank editorial. Who owns this newspaper?"

"I forget the man's name, but he's mysteriously rich and there are stories he has underground connections with the Family back East."

"And I thought we'd get away from that sort of thing out here." Jeremy sighed.

"It's monstrous!" cried Tash.

"What did you expect? *Hic draconis.*"

"Meaning?"

"Dragon Land. The words written in the unexplored spaces on medieval maps. No matter how far we travel today, we are still in Minotaur Country, where anything can happen."

"There's one other thing," said Carlos. "A last minute change in our itinerary. You can't speak at Catclaw Falls this afternoon, because there was a flash flood there this morning. All the roads are under water now and there's no airport. The railway doesn't even go there. Shall we just spend the day loafing here and go on this evening to your last meeting at the jet port?"

"Seems a pity to waste a whole day." Jeremy frowned. "Why can't we go to that place we had to cross off the itinerary for lack of time? The place you wrote me about where a river flows around mountain tops."

"It's a bit late to organize a meeting for this afternoon," said Carlos. "But I'll get on the telephone and see what I can do."

He came back smiling.

"All set. They were really pleased. We're announcing the change of venue on television now so people who want to come to the meeting will have time to change their plans."

169

The road had been ascending steadily ever since they left the mountain inn. By noon they were in still higher country with mile after mile of evergreens along the road, pine and spruce, larch and fir. A carpet of dead needles made it impossible for undergrowth to flourish. This was the fairy-tale wood of a child's dream, where you could see the woods for the trees. Slender trunks stood in serried ranks like soldiers at attention.

The sun had just set, but it was not yet dark enough to turn on the headlights when they rounded a cliffside and came upon a crowd of several hundred people gathered at a crossroads. Beyond this small open space was an impossible view: a river, plunging, powerful and turbulent around a sharp bend in its course, forcing its way between two mountain tops where it had no business to be.

"This is the place you wrote me about," said Jeremy to Carlos. "Incredible! But that water's noisy. Do I have to speak outdoors?"

"No, there's a clubhouse. We're coming to it now."

It was a large building but primitive—simple board and batten walls with a shingled roof and a few steps leading up to the front door.

Inside it was dark. The windows were narrow and the unshaded bulbs in fixtures along the walls could not disperse the dusk. Folding chairs were arranged in rows with an aisle in the middle. There was a dais for speakers at the farther end with a table and chairs and in one corner an old, upright piano. The table was furnished with two drinking glasses and a carafe of dusty looking water.

It looked to Tash like a place used for Saturday night dances. She was not surprised when she learned later that it had been built to serve as a neighborhood boys' clubhouse.

"No microphone?" said Jeremy to Carlos.

170

"Afraid not, but you've talked without them before."

The crowd from outside filled all the chairs, and there was an overflow of standees at the back of the hall. They were family groups, men, women, and children, all in working clothes, and there were even a few dogs—the working sheep dogs who are so intelligent and devoted.

Carlos and Job, Hilary and Tash followed Jeremy onto the platform and found seats behind the speakers' chairs. Most of the wire service men preferred to stay in the body of the hall, where they could listen to comments in the crowd. The press photographers climbed up to the high window sills where they could get shots of both speakers and audience.

A burly man in work boots and jeans, plaid shirt and Stetson, was introduced to Jeremy by Carlos as Malcolm MacLain, a neighboring rancher, who was to preside at the meeting.

Mr. MacLain was long-winded and repetitive. He addressed himself to the Governor rather than the audience, explaining that it was the first time a governor had ever visited this part of the state, and though it had taken all of them a great deal of time and trouble to get here this evening, they just couldn't let him drive down their road without asking him to stop and say a few words.

He praised Jeremy for everything he had done and several things he hadn't done, and then, finally, he started winding up to his peroration like a pitcher warming up at the plate, and at long last let his ball go in a stentorian voice:

"And so, ladies and gentlemen, it gives me great pleasure to introduce to you His Excellency the Governor of this state, Jeremy Playfair."

Wild clapping, hooraying, and stamping from an audience which must have found any excuse for exercise a relief after sitting still for so long.

Jeremy rose, smiling, looking slender and boyish beside the burly rancher, standing with an ease and grace peculiarly his own.

His light baritone voice was relaxed and informal, perfectly at home. It was not "raised" or "projected" yet it carried to every corner of the room.

"What can I say after an introduction like that?"

The smile and the two-edged meaning of the words won his audience immediately. As he saw he had their sympathy, he went on swiftly and happily with a glancing reference now and then to the planks in his official platform. He was halfway through that list, when he was interrupted.

"What about the two guys killed during the dock strike? Why didn't you settle it before anyone was killed?"

There are only two ways of dealing with a heckler: You can ignore him and sweep on with your speech, hoping to carry the audience with you; or you can put him down with a stroke of wit so stunning that it stops his mouth long enough to give the audience a chance to laugh and forget him.

Answering a heckler at length is as hopeless as a motorist arguing with a traffic cop or an author answering a book reviewer. In all combat the advantage is with the one who has the power to attack.

Jeremy was known for his skill as a debater. Time and again in his political campaigns, he had been inspired with a quip so light and yet so lethal that it had disarmed a heckler, but tonight inspiration failed him. Was he just tired? Did he blame himself for the deaths of the two men who might have lived if he had been able to settle the strike sooner? Was he still suffering more than he himself had realized from the shock of the fire and the enigma of Vivian's death?

Whatever the reason, he chose to go on with his speech as if there had been no interruption.

172

Sometimes it works. This time it didn't.

"We have the satisfaction now of improved relations with Barlovento—"

"Commies, ain't they? Friends of yours?"

The same voice from the same part of the hall.

Heads turned in that direction.

Where Jeremy stood, he could not see the man, but he knew he had to answer now. A second interruption cannot be ignored.

"Would anyone here have preferred a war in the Caribbean? That was the alternative to the decision we made."

"Sez you! You're pro-Barlo. You've even got one of them working for you now."

"Mr. de Miranda is an American citizen."

"Any spy can take out papers!"

Jeremy stepped to the front of the dais. "Why don't you come down here in front where everyone can see you as well as hear you?"

The reply was inaudible.

Why didn't Jeremy take advantage of that to go on with his speech? Apparently, he felt that the heckler's insinuations were too serious to slide away from, for he said:

"I can't hear you."

The answer was clear enough: "Then I'll come closer."

Now every pair of eyes in the room, including Jeremy's were fixed on the little ripple in the crowd where someone unseen was trying to push his way through from the back.

Tash, sitting on one side of the dais near the edge, had a clearer view of Jeremy and those in the front rows near him than anyone else. She caught her breath.

Hilary, beside her, said, "What's wrong?"

Tash could only stare at the place where she had seen

173

a figure pass under the light from one of the bulbs near the front and melt into the shadow beyond. The blind-looking eyes and elfin smile were unmistakable. Why was Freaky here, so far from his urban habitat?

Others had marked his progress through the crowd. Now, as he stepped beyond the first row and stood alone and conspicuous looking up at the dais, every eye was on him, watching to see what he would do next.

The explosion was so unexpected in that context that no one identified it immediately.

Hilary said, "That sounded like a shot, but it can't be."

Job's face was a mask of shock and terror: staring eyes, slack jaw, bloodless cheeks.

Tash looked at Jeremy. He was still standing, but Carlos was holding him up, and his head had fallen forward.

She had only the dimmest awareness of other people shouting and pushing as she forced her way to his side.

His eyes were closed. There was only a little blood on his face. It was Carlos, unharmed and fully aware of what had happened, who looked like death.

She took one of Jeremy's hands. It lay in hers, inert and unfeeling.

"We must get an ambulance!" shouted Wilkes.

"There isn't time," said Carlos.

"Then we must get him to a car, any car. Pulaski, clear a path to the door."

"But the man who fired the shot . . . ?"

"Leave him to the others."

Tash followed. No one tried to stop her. She got into the back seat beside Jeremy and took his head in her lap. Carlos was driving. He was the only one who had been here before and knew the road. Wilkes and Pulaski crowded into the front seat beside him.

Tash used a handkerchif to wipe away the blood on Jeremy's face. She remembered that people in shock must be kept warm. Someone had left an overcoat on the floor of the car. She pulled it over him, and kissed his forehead. It was not cold. It was just without warmth the way inanimate things are.

The hospital was on the outskirts of a small city. There was a red light over the emergency entrance and a young intern waiting there.

"Someone telephoned us to be ready for a man who was shot. He said it was the Governor. But who would—"

"Hurry!"

Jeremy was put on a stretcher with wheels. Tash followed it into an elevator. On the fourth floor it was pushed down the corridor to a pre-surgery room.

The intern looked at Tash. "You'll have to wait here, ma'am."

She stood and watched them wheel the stretcher away. Doors closed after it.

A nurse came out of another elevator. "Miss Perkins? There are some reporters downstairs—"

"I'll talk to them," said Carlos.

Tash found chairs at the other end of the hall and sat down.

"Tea? Coffee?" said the nurse.

She shook her head.

The chair was uncomfortable. She looked down and saw blood had stained the robin's egg blue of her skirt. So it really was happening. You couldn't imagine bloodstains that real.

She did not know how long she had waited when she heard a step and looked up to see Carlos again.

"Any word?"

She shook her head.

He sat down beside her. "It was clever. The heckler to distract us so everybody was looking his way and no one saw who fired the shot."

"I know who the heckler was," said Tash. "Freaky. He

used the same trick when Halcòn picked my pocket. Diversion, misdirection."

After a while Carlos persuaded Tash to lie down on a couch and close her eyes. She could almost feel time crawling by, second after second, minute after minute, the unendurable that had to be endured.

Footsteps and a murmur of voices. She opened her eyes. One look at Carlos' face told her everything.

She whispered: "No . . ."

A long time afterward, they were driving through a cold, gray dawn. The car had to stop when it came to a place in the road cordoned off by state police.

"You might have taken her around another way." The voice was Hilary's.

She heard Carlos answer. "There is no other way."

She looked beyond the little knot of state troopers and reporters and curiosity seekers to mountain peaks and a river flowing around a curve between two of them.

She spoke to the trooper who was driving.

"Does this place have a name?"

"Yes, ma'am. It's called Desolation Bend."

PART IV

Cayo Siesta

16

INSHORE, THE SEA was Egyptian blue, brilliant as newly mined turquoise, a blue with green undertones. Outshore, it was the deep, clear, acid-looking green of jewel jade. The roads were cut out of white coral rock, and the blocks dug out were used to build houses. The fine, white sand of the beaches was powdered coral tinged sometimes with the faintest blush of pink. When you saw a spray of pink oleander blossom against the improbable seascape, the first reaction was simply: I don't believe it! How could Nature, so gray and circumspect in the north, cut loose with the exuberant vulgarity of a picture postcard the moment she came south?

The hibiscus, carefully cultivated as a small pink flower in the gardens of Leafy Way, was a big splash of red growing wild along the ditches here.

You didn't go to a florist for gardenias here, or to a grocer for lemons. You picked both from your own bush or tree, where they flourished among passion flowers and night-blooming cereus, gold trees and orchids and bougainvillea.

In your orchard were guavas and mangoes, persimmons and pomegranates, papaya and *monstera deliciosa*.

It was not only the vegetable world that flourished.

There were bold palm rats that could swim across an inlet and flying cockroaches that ate clothes. Spiders here were big as a man's fist and might drop on your head or shoulder from the ceiling at any moment. There were coral snakes for whom anti-venin was kept in every house. There were fleas so prolific that if dogs brought them onto your wall-to-wall carpet you had to analyze their breeding cycle before you could get rid of them. There was heart worm that killed dogs without warning. There were virus diseases that struck you with an exuberant will to live at your expense, which no well behaved northern virus ever displayed.

Even in the sea there were colonial organisms like the Portuguese man-of-war, which looked more like a gaudy plastic toy than anything alive, but whose sting could put you in the hospital for days. And in deep water there were always the sharks.

In short, the eternal sun that so invigorated you and your species also invigorated all the other species that preyed on you and yours. What Nature gave with one hand, she took away with the other. The Miranda family had adapted to all this generations ago, mimimizing the disadvantages and enjoying the advantages without any distortion of their ideals. Sun and rum might act like adrenalin on cruise tourists and tax evaders from the north, but over the rest of the island there still brooded the amiable spirit of Granada and Algeciras.

Cayo Siesta was the largest island in the Sotavento group and shaped like a crescent. The Casa Miranda was on one tip of that crescent. If you wanted to go to town, your shortest route was to take a launch in a straight line across the bay instead of going the long way around the crescent by car.

The house itself reflected a Spanish tradition that goes back to the days when Iberia was a Roman colony. It was built around a true patio with house walls on all four sides, a cloister along each inner wall, and a fountain in the middle of the patio.

Outside, the house was like a fortress with barred windows and high double carriage doors of heavy mahogany.

Inside, the patio was an outdoor room with only the sky for its ceiling, yet guarded from all observation by the walls of the house itself. Persian roses and Persian peaches grew along the walls. Carp swam in the basin around the fountain. Its plashing made a cool tinkle on the hottest day.

What more could anyone want than this lotus-eating life? A plunge in cold surf before breakfast, a ride along the beach on a pure-bred Arab mare before luncheon, another swim and then a long afternoon in the sun reading and sipping a chilled rum drink while faint music came from the stereo in one of the cloisters.

Why had Carlos left all this to get himself into the North American merry-go-round?

Carlos seemed to read her thoughts. "In time you get tired of it," he said one afternoon.

"Why?"

A shrug. "Not enough conflict."

"That's the very thing that appeals to me now." Tash realized she was getting close to the things they didn't talk about and veered away quickly. "*Cay* or *cayo* in Spanish and *quai* in French, but key in English. I wonder why?"

"Because in the eighteenth century key was pronounced 'kay' in English, just as tea was pronounced 'tay' and still is in Ireland. It should be Kay West, not Key West."

Felipe, who ran the household here as efficiently as the chief usher had run Leafy Way, came across the patio to Tash with a cablegram.

"Oh, dear! My mother and father will be here to-night."

"Why does that bother you? We have plenty of room."

"Your mother has been kindness itself, but . . . they're divorced, you know."

"I've told her all about it. She is looking forward to meeting them, and so am I."

At the airport, it seemed to Tash that both her parents were wearing their "everything-is-going-to-be-all-right" masks.

"Darling Tash!" Her mother's mask did not slip, but it quivered, and for the first time Tash began to realize what anguish both her parents must have gone through when news flashed around the world that she had been so close to Jeremy Playfair when he was killed. She could so easily have died with him.

"And this is Mr. de Miranda?" her father was saying. "How very kind of you to have us here. I don't know if this is good or bad news, but you've got another guest coming whom we met on the plane, a Captain Wilkes."

"Ted!" Carlos called out as he saw Wilkes approaching "I hope you've come for a real vacation?"

"Only twenty-four hours," said Wilkes. "I have to go back tomorrow. And it's not a vacation. I've been fired, or, at least, asked to resign by Governor Jackman."

Tash turned away from the others to hide her face. Governor Jackman. Of course. As lieutenant governor, Job would succeed Jeremy automatically, and his first act in office would be to ask for Wilkes' resignation. Job would never forgive poor Wilkes for what had happened at Desolation Bend.

"And how is Job?" asked Hilary.

"Bitter. His whole future was geared to promoting Governor Playfair at the national level. Now that's gone, and he's floundering hopelessly in the job of governor.

182

After he serves out the rest of Playfair's term, he'll probably retire from politics. He's just not the type who can run for high office on his own and hope to be elected. His only chance lay in being the tail of other candidate's comet, and now he's lost that."

Mariquita de Miranda, white-haired and grave, received the northern strangers with unshakable dignity and introduced Carlos' younger sisters, Eulalia and Manuela, as imperturbably as if unexpected guests arrived at twelve hours' notice or less every day of her life. Watching her, Tash realized how much of Carlos' character had been formed by his mother. The devotion of Spanish sons to their mothers was famous throughout Europe.

Over before-dinner sherry in the patio, the party split up into smaller groups, and Tash found herself with Wilkes and Carlos.

"You can't blame Jackman for asking me to resign," said Wilkes to Carlos. "In his place, I'd have done the same thing. After all, I was in charge."

"What, will happen now?" asked Tash.

"I don't know, but I'm afraid my successor is going to arrest the wrong man. That's why I'm here."

"How can we help?"

"By letting me talk. If we pool information and ideas, we may think of something that will lead us to the real murderer."

Carlos strolled over to a television set in one corner of the cloister. "Let's find out what's happening now."

"You're too early, Carlito!" said Eulalia, with a trace of sisterly discipline. "The news doesn't come on until eight."

"Which will give us plenty of time to get sound and picture adjusted before it comes on," said Carlos with a trace of brotherly rebellion.

As a courtesy to his guests, Carlos turned on a broadcast in English, so they all understood the big news of the evening when it came just before dinner.

"We interrupt this program with a news flash from the mainland. A former citizen of Barlovento, known to the police as Halcón, and wanted for questioning about the assassination of Governor Playfair, has just been shot and killed by police here while resisting arrest. The new Governor, Job Jackman, deplored the fact that Halcón can now never be brought to trial. The police officers who shot him are now under arrest pending investigation. . . ."

"Halcón!" Wilkes' face was tight as a clenched fist. "That's the man I was talking about. The wrong man. He never killed the Governor."

Nothing more was said until Carlos' mother and sisters had left the patio. Eulalia and Manuela would have lingered had not their mother's firm voice indicated her displeasure at the very thought of such a possibility.

Tash's parents were never slow to take a hint. They pleaded jet fatigue and followed the Miranda women into the shadows of the cloister.

"I admire your mother," said Tash to Carlos. "She has her daughters well in hand."

"For how long? Next autumn they go to college on the mainland."

"Of course they must if they are to survive in the kind of world we shall all have to live in. At least they'll start out with a moral sense."

Tash smiled. "I'm not worried about their morals. I'm I'm just afraid they'll lose their charming manners."

Wilkes stood under the gold tree, a glass of brandy in one hand. "He wasn't a nice character."

"Who?" asked Hilary.

"Halcón. A thief, a pusher, a pimp, and a heroin ad-

184

dict. Yet, for that very reason, I don't believe he shot Governor Playfair. The Family does not entrust the art of assassination to petty hopheads. Hitmen are the most specialized of all criminals, highly paid for their superb marksmanship. Halcón's hands shook so, that he couldn't have hit a barn door at ten paces."

"So it was a fanatic after all!" cried Carlos. "A psycho yielding to a sudden impulse, triggered no doubt by that abusive editorial in the local rag. Editorials like that were published before the assassinations of both McKinley and Kennedy."

"Impulsive?" Wilkes shook his head. "That trick of getting hecklers to dustract the audience from the assassin had to be organized. That implies premeditation. The whole thing had the professional touch—organized, swift, accurate, anonymous. Only the Family could have supplied the human weapon that fired that shot, but I'm not interested in him. I want the man who really killed the Governor, the man who got the Family to do it.

"Halcón must have known who that man was, but now Halcón himself is dead. He'll never be cross-examined now. We'll never know what he knew. That's a Family technique. Get rid of your victim first, and then get rid of any witnesses. 'Resisting arrest!' The classic pretext."

"Did the newscast say who actually fired the shot that killed Halcón?" asked Hilary.

"No. They said there was a scuffle when Halcón was being moved from one cell to another. Several guns went off. Ballistics will identify one of them. If I were there, I should look for some cop who had got just a little too close to the rackets and laid himself open to blackmail.

"The real killer must be feeling safe tonight. The public has seen a scapegoat sacrificed, and the Playfair case will now go into a file marked *Closed.*"

"And what has become of Freaky?" asked Tash.

"Vanished as if he had never existed. That also suggests professionals with safe houses and underground escape routes just like a spy network."

"It's another world," said Hilary. "A shadow world as dark and remote from ours as the other side of the moon."

"Not as remote as you might think," retorted Wilkes. "Our vices still finance it as they did during Prohibition. Mrs. Playfair's drug habit was one link between the two worlds, and there are many other more important links, financial and political. The underworld reverses our world and so proves that it is a reflection of our world, a mirror-image. It stands still only when we stand still. It moves only when we move."

Tash was watching Wilkes' face. "A penny for your real thoughts. You haven't come so far just to tell us things like that."

"You won't like my thoughts."

"Try us," said Carlos. "We may be more broad-minded than you think."

"At first glance, this case is like a cliff without a hand-hold or even a toehold for the climber," said Wilkes. "But, even on the blankest cliffside, a determined mountaineer can usually find one or two toeholds, however slight."

"And you have found some?" cried Tash.

"Just one. And it is only acceptable if we assume three things we haven't proved. First, that the killing of Halcón was the killing of a scapegoat by some agent of the Family in order to protect the real murderer of Governor Playfair. Second, that Mrs. Playfair's death was murder, too."

"I knew it all along!" exclaimed Tash. "I had warned her about keeping an ashtray on her bed with a burning cigarette in it. She'd promised she'd stop. I knew she meant it from the way she said it. If she was being as careful as that, I don't see how the fire could have started accidentally. It was arson, and it was meant to kill her and Jeremy both. He only escaped because he was with me, and the murderer couldn't have anticipated that."

"What is your third assumption?" asked Hilary.

"That both murders were planned by someone intimately associated with the Governor and Mrs. Playfair."

"And the toehold?" prompted Carlos.

"I've found out why the fire alarm didn't go off in time the night of the fire. We missed the reason because it was so obvious, right in front of our eyes, and we were looking for something hidden and subtle.

"You recall the penny that was found in Miss Perkins' office after the dead canary was left on her typewriter? And the dimes found in Mrs. Playfair's room after the fire?"

"Yes, but . . ."

"Have you all forgotten that a coin will blow a fuse and cut out any electrical circuit, including the one that powers an alarm system? If you are able to put a new fuse in the fuse box afterward, there will be no evidence to show what has happened."

"Of course!" said Tash. "Carlos, I remember your telling me that we had an old-fashioned alarm system at Leafy Way with no long-term batteries to back it up if current went off during a storm."

"Simple, isn't it?" said Wilkes. "As you know, each floor at Leafy Way had its own fuse box, and each suite of rooms its own alarm system with its own circuit. How easy to blow a fuse, knock out a circuit, and leave the alarm in one suite off long enough for the fire to get out of control and spread. Then replace the fuse, so the alarm will go off too late to be of any use as a warning, but early enough to keep people from realizing that the alarm must have been turned off temporarily when the fire started. Its delayed reaction would be put down to some flaw in the mechanism."

"Wouldn't it have been even simpler to set and reset the alarm buttons?" suggested Hilary.

"To do that, you'd have to find out the combination. There was a different one for each suite of rooms. Much easier to bypass all that and simply control one of the alarm systems through its power source."

"There's one thing I don't understand," said Tash. "Short-circuiting an alarm inside the house could only be done by someone already inside."

"Exactly. It was an inside job."

"And the alarm was short-circuited by the same person who let Freaky in and out?"

"Obviously. The Family must be involved, but the murders were made possible by someone in the Governor's own household. He was betrayed by someone he trusted."

Carlos' dark eyes blazed. "Are you suggesting . . . ?"

Wilkes said, "Nothing. Nothing at all."

And walked out of the patio.

"This is intolerable!" cried Carlos. "A guest in my own house who—"

"Who is trying to find Jeremy's murderer," said Hilary. "We've got to help him. After all, it's only for a few hours more. He did say he was going back to the mainland."

"He'd better! He has insulted my guests and me. You may help him if you like, but I shall leave the house now and not return until he has gone."

"I feel the same way, Carlos," said Tash. "I shall get a headache tomorrow morning and stay in bed so I don't have to see him again before he goes."

She was half asleep when her mother came into her room to say good-night. They talked of nothing for a few moments, and then her mother said, "You were in love with him, weren't you?"

Tash nodded.

"Dear girl, you must make a clean break, Come to me in Boston, or go to your father in Rome, but don't try to go on living where you knew him."

"Running away?"

"What's wrong with running away if it saves life or reason? Unnecessary heroism is just vanity."

She didn't have to invent a headache. She awoke at seven with a sore throat and a slight fever.

Mariquita de Miranda took one look at her and said, "I am going to take everybody out in the launch for an excursion to the other islands so you can go back to sleep. Carlos has gone off by himself somewhere, so you'll have the house to yourself all day."

Tash awoke again at nine feeling better but still without appetite. She could tell from the silence that no one else was about. Felipe and the rest of the staff must be in their own quarters.

In such stillness her thoughts could range free over many things without distraction. The slight fever seemed to spur them to wander further afield than they had gone before.

Carlos, Job, Hilary, the three people in Jeremy's household who had been closest to him—three people she had liked and trusted, but suspicion, once planted in the mind, grows perversely with the unwanted strength of a weed.

She could not see a motive for any one of them, Carlos, loyal friend and perfect ADC, Hilary who loved Jeremy as a son, Job, whose whole life was a scaffolding built to support Jeremy's future career.

How could a treacherous friend bear to be present at the end? Could it be that Job's quick trip to Washington was an attempt to escape that? No, Job was away August 8th, Jeremy died September 9th. The dates were too far apart to be confused.

What about Wilkes himself?

There were corrupt policemen. He himself had said that a security system is only as strong as its weakest human link. The mere fact that Halcón was said to have been shot by police while resisting arrest suggested police involvement. Jeremy himself had not trusted Wilkes enough to ask him for help with Vivian's drug problem. By coming down to Sotavento, Wilkes had given himself an alibi for the actual shooting of Halcón, but he might have planned it. Who was in a better position than Wilkes to make contact with petty criminals like Halcón and Freaky? As a policeman, he dealt with such people every day. Did Job suspect him? Was that the real reason Job had fired him? Had Wilkes discussed the case last night because he wanted to find out if any of them suspected him?

He was in a unique position to stay close to the investigation. All the policemen who had worked with him before his downfall would talk to him freely about the case. They might even ask him for help or advice. That would put him in an ideal position to turn suspicion away from himself if it veered in his direction.

It wouldn't occur to any of them that he himself might be involved. He had not been dismissed. Job had allowed him to resign. What else could Job do if there was no evidence against him? No doubt, there had been an exchange of polite letters published in the newspapers. Everyone would sympathize with Wilkes because he had happened to be in charge of the Governor's security when the Governor was killed through no apparent fault of Wilkes.

Who could possibly imagine that the man responsible for Jeremy's safety was the man who had arranged for Jeremy's murder? Yet who had a better opportunity to do so?

And now Wilkes was leaving Cayo Siesta in a few hours. She might never be so close to him again. Could there possibly be some clue, some indication of the truth in the things he had brought with him? She would never have a chance to find out again.

Of course, a cop turned crook would be even more cunning and knowledgeable than a professional crook in hiding his traces and getting rid of things that might incriminate him as he went along, like a tidy housewife washing her pots and pans after each step in her cooking. And yet . . .

All humanity is fallible, expecially criminal humanity with its great psychological burden of guilt. He just might have overlooked something.

Barefoot, in shirt and shorts, she went down the arcade that led to his room, silent as a ghost.

The suitcase was empty. In the bureau drawers there were only nightclothes and underclothes. In the old-fashioned wardrobe, nothing but the slacks and jacket he had worn when he got off the plane.

Her disappointment made her realize how much she had counted on the possibility of finding something. Now she had to face the probability that her theory about Wilkes was all wrong, and that made her heartily ashamed of herself for having searched his room. In future she would leave detection to the police.

She went back to the patio and looked about for a book to read. She was sure she had seen some on the coffee table that morning. She remembered thinking: Someone will have to bring them in if it rains. And then she had realized that it hardly ever rained in Sotavento at this time of year.

The books were still there. She picked up the one on top of the others, and from its pages a piece of paper fluttered to the ground. Apparently, it had been used as a bookmark.

As she picked up the paper to put it back in the book, she glanced at it and froze.

She sat down to look at it more carefully.

It was a letter in Spanish from someone in Madrid, a letter handwritten in a smoothly flowing, stylish script as clear as print.

> Calle de Valencia, 100,
> Madrid, Espana.
> 10–6–71

Dear Carlos,

> We eagerly anticipate your visit, but please let us know when you expect to reach the airport, so I can make proper arrangements to meet your plane.
>> Your devoted cousin,
>> Saturnino.

She read the first four lines again.

Why had they caught her eye? What was wrong with them?

Suddenly, she knew.

She put the letter in her pocket. Carlos would never miss an old scrawl he had used as a bookmark. Even if he did, it no longer mattered now.

She went to the telephone and tried to make a person-to-person call to Bill Brewer. She heard his secretary's voice tell the operator he wasn't there and no one knew where he was.

She called the airport. The quickest route was a local plane from Cayo Siesta to Miami, a jet from Miami to Washington, and another local plane to her own city.

192

If she could catch the plane for Miami that left Cayo Siesta at eleven, she could go straight through without delays and reach her destination around five-thirty.

She didn't stop to pack, but she scribbled a short note.

Dear Carlos,

Something desperately important has come up. I must leave for the States at once. I can't even wait to say good-bye to your mother or I'll miss my plane. Please forgive me and apologize for me, and tell everybody I'll be back to explain myself in a day or so.

Yours,
Tash.

She rang for Felipe and gave him the note.

"Can you run me over to the airport in a car, or shall I get a taxi?"

"A car is at your service, señorita."

Thirty minutes later, she was airborne.

In Washington there was no plane available, so she went on by train.

In the dingy, old railway station, she found a pay telephone and called Bill's office again. She knew she could not handle this alone, and she was counting on Bill's help, but he was still out.

"I'm sorry, Miss Perkins," said the secretary. "But he's been out all afternoon. No, I don't know when he'll be back, but why don't you try again later?"

"Because I need to talk to him now. Have you no telephone number where he could be reached?"

"No, he didn't leave one. You want to leave a message?"

So she would have to handle it alone after all.

She looked resentfully at the telephone as if it were at

fault. "All right. Please ask him to call Tatiana Perkins at 742–6539 when he comes in."

A taxi took her to the garage she used in town.

When she drove out, the sun was low in the west, casting a liquid, golden light over roof tops, leaving streets below in a blue dusk.

She crossed the main thoroughfare, turned left, and was soon on the long, winding road to Fox Run.

PART V

Further Lane

17

WHEN SHE CAME to the place in the road where woods gave way to open meadow, she stopped the car.

It was the same hour of late afternoon when she first saw this house, the day she and Hilary had been surprised on the lawn by Jeremy and Carlos just back from Sotavento.

How strange that the past, so vivid in memory, no longer existed in fact. Where did the past go? Why couldn't she find her way back to it?

It had been Jeremy's fancy that this lane was called Further Lane, instead of Farther Lane, because it led somewhere in time rather than space. If only it did . . .

She started the car again and turned down the driveway toward the tall, angular house, sitting on its grassy knoll among shade trees, surrounded by fields.

The first change she noticed was an ugly wire-mesh fence between the road and the house, probably electrified. The second was the fact that the sentry didn't recognize her. A stranger in uniform examined her press card and driver's license, and telephoned to the guard room before he finally let her pass.

A new chief usher greeted her politely enough at the door and showed her into one of the reception rooms on the north side of the house, away from the garden.

All signs of Jeremy's personal presence were gone. This was Job Jackman's house once more, simple, solid, unimaginative.

Jo Beth was the first to put in an appearance.

"Tash, dear, it's been so long!" A double handclasp, a quick, dry kiss on one cheek. "But you're looking well!" Jo Beth stood back and surveyed the suntan with a touch of envy. "Sotavento agreed with you. What will you have now? Tea or a drink?"

"Tea, please."

"Just what I'd like myself."

As she touched a bell, one of her boys came into the room.

"You know Greg, don't you?"

"I don't believe I do." Tash smiled at him. "But I've heard so much about you from your mother, I feel as if we were old friends."

He smiled with a touch of shyness, but he wasn't too shy. He talked freely and pleasantly. Whatever was eccentric in Job had not come down to him. Given enough time, genes would always tend to pull back to the norm of the species.

Job came in as they were finishing tea, and the boy had the tact to excuse himself. Job did not look like a governor now, any more than he ever had, but he was behaving like one.

"Your papers are still in your desk, Tash, just as you left them," he said. "I didn't know what you wanted to do with them."

"There's nothing important," she answered. "If someone will throw them all in a carton and send them over to my apartment, I can sort them out there."

"Are you home for good?"

"I don't know."

"Then I'll have the carton delivered right away."

"Before long, we'll have to start our own packing," said Jo Beth. "I'd much rather stay here in our own home, but Job feels we should move into Leafy Way as soon as we can."

"When will Leafy Way be ready?"

"They say a month now. Knowing contractors, that probably means two or three months."

Tash turned back to Job. "There's something I'd like to ask you: Are the police satisfied, now, that Halcón is the man responsible for Jeremy's death?"

"Of course. Do you doubt it?"

"Captain Wilkes came down to Sotavento."

"That troublemaker! He's driven by his sense of guilt. It was his job to protect Jeremy, and he failed."

"It may not have been solely his fault."

"What do you mean?"

"He has some new ideas about all this. I came here today because I thought I ought to pass them along to the police through you."

"And what are they?" Job smiled indulgently as one smiles at a precocious, but pre-logical child.

"He doesn't believe that Vivian's death was an accident. He believes that someone deliberately short-circuited the fire alarm and replaced the burnt-out fuse half an hour later, so the alarm wouldn't go off until the fire was out of control."

Job was no longer smiling.

"That could only be done by someone inside the house."

"That's just what Captain Wilkes says. He believes Jeremy was betrayed by someone he trusted in his own household."

"Can he prove it?"

"I don't know."

199

Job was no longer smiling.

"Not a nice thought. When will Wilkes be back?"

"Tomorrow."

"What would you think about my appointing him as a special prosecutor? He's a lawyer as well as a policeman."

"That's a good idea. He'd give anything to solve this case, just because he feels guilty."

"Then why did he resign?"

"Didn't you ask him to?"

"No."

"He seemed to think you expected it."

"I didn't."

"He must have misunderstood something you said."

Job and Jo Beth walked with Tash as far as the hall.

"What became of that Chinese painting, *Dragon Playing with a Pearl*?" she asked.

"Carlos gave orders before he left for Sotavento that all Jeremy's personal things should be packed and stored until his heirs could get here."

"Who are his heirs?"

"Some distant cousins, I believe. Sad, isn't it? Jeremy should have had children."

"Yes." Tash repeated the words. "Jeremy should have had children. And now, I must say good-bye."

"Can I reach you at your apartment in the next few days?" asked Job.

"Oh, yes, I'll stay there until Wilkes' questions are answered."

"And where will you go then?"

"Anywhere except here."

Compassion stole into Jo Beth's eyes, and she ventured a little nearer the edge of all the things they had left unsaid.

"I hope things work out for you. I shall think of you

often, and I hope you will always think of me as a friend. We were Jeremy's people, and we should hang together now he's gone. We are the only ones who know how many hopes were buried with him."

"I'll call you as soon as I've talked to Wilkes," said Job. "I suppose you're on your way home now?"

"Yes, but I'm going to stop first at the beach."

"At the beach! Why?"

She couldn't say, because that's the place where Jeremy first kissed me. So she simply said: "Good-bye!" and ran down the steps to her car.

Further Lane ended where the last of its macadam rose up a steep incline to the crest of a sandy hill.

Tash stopped the car at the very edge of the macadam, close to three tall, old pine trees with trunks almost as thick as a man's waist. She shut off the engine, shifted gear, and sat still, listening to the steady pounding of the surf.

Beyond white horses you could see a choppy ocean flecked with foam as far as the horizon. The twilight was gray, the color of dreams; under that bleak sky, the sea was slate-blue. Hard to believe that only a thousand miles or so to the south that same ocean was jade and turquoise.

She glanced at her watch. She had been here ten minutes.

She ought to go now.

Suppose Bill Brewer was trying to return her call?

Still, she sat without moving and listened to the wild keening of the gulls and watched a sandpiper flicking along the wet edge of the beach.

Why not get out and walk down to the sea that Jeremy had so loved?

She stood still beside the open door of the car, resting one hand on its wide handle while she looked up at the skyscape she had been unable to see from under the roof of the car.

Each cloud was a different shade of gray, from iron to pewter to dove color, all overlapping and all moving, languidly, almost imperceptibly.

She did not hear a sound behind her, but she felt a sudden, gentle nudge from the car door standing open close beside her. The next thing she knew, searing pain darted through her chest. The car had rolled backward a little way downhill, but it had been forced to stop when the heavy, open door pinned her against the huge trunk of the nearest pine tree.

That tree and her body kept the car from rolling farther, the way big stones wedged under the rear wheels will keep a car from rolling backward downhill. Her shoulders and upper arms were clamped and crushed between tree trunk and car door as in a giant vise. She could not move and she did not try to twist herself sidewise into a more comfortable position. If her body took up less room between tree and door, the car might roll again. It needed only a few inches more and she would be crushed to death.

How could the car roll? Hadn't she set the automatic gear shift on *P* for *park* when he got out?

She tried to retrieve a visual memory of the gauge as she had last seen it, but nothing came. That meant she had not looked at the gauge when she got out of the car, so she could have left it in neutral instead of park. She remembered Job scolding her for doing that very thing one morning long ago when her car had rolled in the driveway at Leafy Way.

Was there nothing she could do?

Just stand as still as she possibly could to keep the car from rolling farther, and hang onto sanity somehow until somebody came.

But who would come to a lonely beach in October when night was falling? Did anyone know she was here?

Job and Jo Beth knew, but they would assume she had gone home by now. They would have no reason to search for her until tomorrow, when someone, perhaps Bill, discovered she was missing.

Could she bear it here alone all night? Would the prolonged pain cause permanent injury? What would happen if she fainted during the night and sagged between door and tree? Would the car roll again?

As the minutes ticked by, the temptation to risk turning in the vise to find a more comfortable position became almost irresistible. In another moment she would have yielded if a voice had not spoken.

"Well, Tash. You've really got yourself in trouble this time."

"Oh, Job! Thank God you're here. Can you release me? Or will you need help?"

She heard footsteps coming around the car, and there he was, a ghost in the deep twilight that was almost night. He stood and looked at her without moving. She began to feel like an insect pinned to a board by a painstaking but unsympathetic entomologist.

At last he spoke, softly.

"Why should I release you?"

18

"Did you push the car?"

"No. I was watching you from an upper floor through binoculars, because I was curious to find out what you were going to do at the beach. There was just light enough for me to see what happened, so I walked down by a short cut through the woods to see if you were dead, but you're not. It's a pity the car didn't roll a little farther. We'll have to do something about that."

"You killed Jeremy and Vivian."

"Of course. I always hated them."

"But Jeremy did so much for you!"

"He did nothing for me. Do you think it's fun to play second fiddle all the time? Do you think it's fun to be the power behind the throne and never sit on the throne yourself? Jeremy and Vivian were born to everything I had to struggle for. They took all the rights and privileges I never had for granted. Because they had never known privation, they gambled with opportunities I would have died rather than risk.

"Vivian could have had anything, done anything, gone anywhere. She had everything I ever wanted, and she threw it all away as if it weren't worth having."

"Maybe it wasn't," said Tash.

"How do you know? You've never had to go without

anything you really wanted, have you?" Job took silence for consent and went on: "I knew something was wrong with Vivian, but I didn't know what. It was a shock when I found out she was taking drugs, the kind of thing you associate with kids brutalized by war or the ghetto, not with ladies living at Leafy Way.

"If the newspapers had got hold of that story, it would have destroyed me through Jeremy. WIFE OF GOVERNOR WHO SIGNED BILL SOFT ON ADDICTS TAKES DRUGS HERSELF. She was blithely risking my future and Jeremy's, and for what? Kicks. And His Excellency, head in the clouds as usual, didn't even know what was going on!"

"How did you find out?"

"I saw her coming out of the office of a doctor who has been under suspicion for some time. She couldn't go to any doctor's office often without starting rumors of serious illness sure to reach Jeremy eventually. So how did she usually communicate with her source of drugs? She couldn't go through the switchboard at Leafy Way. She couldn't use the mails regularly without exciting Hilary's curiosity. She couldn't go on such an errand in her own car or a taxi. What could she do? She could ask innocent visitors who came to Leafy Way to mail letters for her.

"I didn't believe it even then, but I had to find out. I didn't want private detectives, always worrying about losing their licenses. Set an addict to catch an addict. I wanted someone who knew drugs and the drug racket and took drugs himself. I've always had contacts with the fringe of the underworld. They have votes, too, and they understand patronage better than we do. So I found Halcón and hired him and his boys to watch Vivian when she went out and intercept any letters that she might be sending out through visitors, by following them and picking their pockets.

"You were the first victim. That letter you carried out

of Leafy Way was addressed to Dr. Grant, the doctor whose office I had seen her leave. She was supposed to be one of his ordinary patients, but she wasn't. That letter contained cash and instructions for delivering the 'package' to her maid, Juana, who would meet his messenger in the old, unguarded right of way, late that night.

"I was afraid to tell Jeremy. Usually, he was the easiest guy in the world to get along with, but if you went against his grain, he could be formidable. I couldn't tell him, but I could shut off her source of drugs, so she would go into withdrawal symptoms. Then even Jeremy would realize what was wrong.

"Of course, I assumed he'd divorce her quietly and then we'd both be safe. She couldn't contest the divorce without the whole truth about her coming out. But even after he knew, he didn't think of divorcing her. I never did understand him.

"Because the letter was intercepted, Vivian did not get the cocaine she expected that night. In a day or so she was frantic enough to risk going to the doctor's office in person once more. From him, she learned that I had threatened him with arrest if he ever supplied her with drugs again.

"I was afraid to have him arrested because it might involve her, but he didn't realize that, so the threat worked. To quiet her frenzy, he gave her one last shot of cocaine, telling her never to come back for more. Because of that shot she was merry and bright during your first luncheon at Leafy Way.

"That soon wore off. He hadn't given her enough. By late afternoon, she was so desperate she took the risk of driving to the doctor's own home in her own car. He was in a panic then. He didn't dare give her more cocaine because of my threats. He gave her some sedative. That's why she came home half-conscious in a half-wrecked car with no memory of what had happened. Jeremy must have begun to distrust Dr. Grant, because he called his own doctor, Henry Clemens, and so learned the truth.

"Of course I was careful to stay away from Leafy Way while all this was going on, but I heard about Vivian's disappearance on television newscasts. I told Halcón to send one of his boys to Juana late that night to find out just what had happened."

So that was why I saw Freaky in the grounds, thought Tash.

"Do you remember His Excellency condescending to tell me that he might not even bother to run for a second term? He knew perfectly well my career would be wrecked if he bowed out, but he was too selfish to care. That was when I first began to wonder if there was any way I could work for myself instead of Jeremy.

"Hilary was always telling me that I could never get elected on my own, that I had no *mana*, whatever that is, that I would never be the star but always the scene-shifter backstage.

"I had believed her, but then, suddenly, I saw a way out. I didn't have to get elected again. I was lieutenant governor. Jeremy was governor. If he died in office, I would succeed him automatically as the next governor without any nonsense about elections."

So it was for this that Jeremy had died. Tash was glad the darkness hid Job's face. She didn't want to see him now.

She couldn't block her ears. His voice went on.

"A governor has more patronage to hand out than any other officer of state. With my knowledge of political back alleys, I needed only a few months to build up the biggest political machine this state has ever seen. Then there would be no limit to what I could do. No limit at all . . .

"Fire is a quick, clean, anonymous way of killing. I

207

thought Juana would be the perfect agent for leaving burning cigarettes on Vivian's bed. Halcón had got her pretty much under his thumb."

"How?"

"He tried bribery, but that didn't work. A few slaps and threats were more effective. She had been tortured before. It was she who switched off the alarm and unlocked a door when Halcón and Freaky searched your office to see if you had any further connection with the drug racket. But after that, something odd happened. She refused to set the fire. When Halcón did it himself, she tried to call for help. He had to kill her."

"I had told her that burning cigarettes and ashtrays were fire hazards on a bed," said Tash. "And Vivian had been kind to her."

But was it really kind to involve Juana in the drug traffic? Or had Vivian been using her just as Job and Halcón had used her?

Job was listening only to his own voice now. He went on as if Tash had not spoken.

"Because Jeremy was a fool about you, he survived the fire. It was then I remembered that the Family hated him as much as I did. He had wrecked their dearest plan when he broke that strike. They had counted on food shortages in Barlovento next winter to start riots. Then they could bring their boy Roya back to restore law and order. Barlovento was a Caribbean Las Vegas when Roya was in power, and the cream of the profits went to the Family.

"They let me use one of their hitmen. I was careful not to have any direct contact with him. I never even saw him or wrote to him. I made all the arrangements through letters to Halcón, and Halcón burned the letters afterward."

So that's why Halcón had to die, thought Tash. The

one man who knew the unmentionable secret that the new Governor had had a hand in the assassination of his predecessor must be destroyed. The Family was equipped to take care situations like that.

"I didn't do any killing," said Job. "I'm not a murderer."

"But you are! If it hadn't been for you, Jeremy would be alive."

"I don't think of it as murder and I shan't think of your death as murder either."

"My death?"

"Would I be talking to you like this if you were going to live? The moment you said Jeremy was betrayed by someone he trusted, I knew you had to die if I was ever to feel safe again. You yourself have made things easy for me. All I have to do now is give your car one more little nudge. Not murder really. Just helping an unfortunate accident along to its logical conclusion. I don't know what a court of law would say—"

A third voice interrupted. "Neither do I, but I can imagine."

Tash cried out: "Oh, Bill . . ." And began to shiver from head to foot.

"And that's all," said Bill Brewer.

"Are you sure?" Captain Wilkes cocked a quizzical eyebrow.

They were sitting in the office where he had been installed as a special prosecutor by a new governor after the arrest and resignation of Job Jackman.

"What do you want to know?"

"Two things: First, how did you happen to arrive on that beach in the nick of time?"

"Tash had called me that afternoon when she got in from Sotavento. She left a number with my secretary, so

209

I could call her back. It was the number of Fox Run, where she expected to be for the next hour or so. Late as it was when I got the message, I called the number. When I found she wasn't there, I asked for Mrs. Jackman, because I knew she and Tash were friends. She said Tash had gone to the beach. That seemed peculiar so late in the evening, and I hadn't much else to do, so I just went along to see what was happening."

"If you hadn't—"

"What's the other question?"

"How did Tash know it was Job Jackman?"

"This is the case of the unnecessary alibi. Job had a perfectly good airtight alibi for August ninth, 1975, when there was no murder, but he had no alibi at all for September eighth 1975, when there was a very terrible murder. Tash wondered if there could be any connection between these two facts.

"Job had gone out of his way to spend August ninth in Washington with the national committee of his party, far from Jeremy and the western tour they were supposed to be making together. It was a day when he didn't need an alibi for anything, so far as Tash knew, but she had a feeling there was something contrived about it, though she couldn't see any motive for contrivance.

"Then, in September, when Jeremy was assassinated, Job had no alibi at all.

"Tash thought about that. Could Job somehow have got those two days mixed, August ninth and September eighth? How could anyone mix them? Did they have anything in common?

"While she was in Sotavento she came across an old letter from Madrid which reminded her that Americans and Europeans do not write numerical dates the same way. She remembered then how Carlos de Miranda, using her numerical birth date for the numbers on her alarm combination at Leafy Way had automatically employed the Spanish numerical date sequence—day-month-year. She had had to reset the combination in the more familiar American numerical date sequence—month-day-year—so she wouldn't forget the combination.

"Not only the Spanish, but all Europeans, even the English, write a numerical date in the day-month-year sequence. Only in America is the month-day-year sequence used."

"I get it!" cried Wilkes. "If an American wrote September 8, 1975, in numerical form, he would write it in the American style, the month-day-year sequence: 9-8-75. But a Spaniard would read that date in the Spanish style, the day-month-year sequence, so to him it would be August 9, 1975.

"Job was always telling us he didn't know a word of Spanish. Halcón was scarcely literate in any language. Between them, a mistake was almost inevitable if they set the date for the assassination by letter as they had to when Job was traveling with the Governor. Telephoning would have been far too risky, and a messenger would have been more dangerous than the mails.

"So Job wasted his carefully contrived alibi on a day when nothing happened, and then, when the assassination did take place, it took him completely by surprise. Tash said that when the shot was fired his face was a mask of shock and terror."

"Why didn't Jackman get in touch with Halcón when nothing happened on August ninth?"

"Any kind of contact with the underworld during that campaign trip, when everyone with the Governor was as much exposed to the glare of publicity as the Governor himself, would have been far too dicey. Remember, reporters were traveling with them all the time."

Wilkes nodded slowly. "And I suppose Halcón wouldn't try to get in touch with Jackman, because Halcón had no reason to think anything was wrong. He would still think he was organizing an assassination for the date he believed Jackman had given him. Even the change of venue to Desolation Bend didn't upset his plan, because it was announced on radio and television twenty-four hours ahead of time. Was it Jackman who thought of controlling the alarm system by shutting its power source off and on?"

"Yes, and it was Jackman who thought of exploiting Mrs. Playfair's habit of smoking in bed to make the fire look like an accident, but he didn't think of everything. It was Freaky's own idea to strangle the canary."

"How is Miss Perkins?"

"Some broken ribs. Some strained ligaments. Nothing that won't heal in a month or so."

"I wonder what will become of her now?"

"Oh, she'll marry and live happily ever after. She's the marrying kind. But I feel sorry for her husband."

"Why?"

"He'll have a rival with whom he'll never be able to compete, Jeremy Playfair."